The Pilgrimage

Practical, energetic Maggie McKinley, seventeen-year-old schoolgirl, becomes involved in the emotional side of life in this latest book in the 'Maggie' series. Maggie is on a cycling tour of the Scottish Highlands with James, her boyfriend, and plans to make a 'pilgrimage' to the glen from which her great-great-granny was evicted at the time of the Clearances. But tensions mount between the two, and Maggie's strong attraction towards a Canadian student she meets, coupled with James's increasing possessiveness, finally brings their relationship to a crisis point.

This is the third book in Joan Lingard's series: a full list of the titles appears overleaf. The author was born in Edinburgh, where she now lives, though she spent most of her childhood and teenage years in Belfast. She wrote six novels for adults before she began to concentrate on children's books, and in addition has written scripts for television.

THE PILGRIMAGE

Joan Lingard

Beaver Books

First published in 1976 by
Hamish Hamilton Children's Books Limited,
90 Great Russell Street, London WD1B 3PT

This paperback edition published in 1981 by
The Hamlyn Publishing Group Limited
London · New York · Sydney · Toronto
Astronaut House, Feltham, Middlesex, England
Third impression 1982

Copyright Text Joan Lingard 1976
ISBN 0 600 20301 8

Printed in England by
Cox & Wyman Limited, Reading
Set in Baskerville

For Bridget, with love

Chapter 1

So many things happened that summer that it's difficult to know where to begin. I might as well start with Catriona Fraser, for what happened to her was dramatic – changed her life and all that – and had an influence over other people's too. Including mine.

Catriona got married. To Alexander. I was flabbergasted when I heard, partly because I had predicted many times that their relationship would not last, and I always expect my instincts to be right, and partly because I had thought that Catriona herself realised how unsuited they were to one another. They had drifted on, seeing each other, being bored, falling out, falling in. And now this! She wrote to tell me they were to be married a week on Saturday and she hoped that James, her brother, and I would come. She did not think that her parents would. It was unlikely since they did not even know!

We were all up in Inverness-shire – not Catriona and Alexander, who were slaving away in a steamy hairdressing salon in Edinburgh – but James and I, and his mother and father. I was staying with my granny and working at the local hotel as a waitress; the Frasers were at their cottage. We had been there for four weeks, and after another two James and I would be heading further north to Easter Ross. We were going on a pilgrimage. To my great-great-granny's glen.

I re-read Catriona's letter five times, trying to read

between the lines, as people claim to be able to do sometimes. There didn't seem to be anything there. 'I am getting married to Alexander. . . .' I couldn't believe it. I examined the back, even the envelope. No messages, in code, or otherwise. No S.W.A.L.K. I giggled. I feel irreverent in most situations.

'Eat up your porridge,' said my granny, 'or you'll no be fit for your work.'

She wouldn't let me out of the house in the mornings until I had eaten a great bowlful of the grey slop she tended so lovingly on the stove from the moment she got up. It was usually full of lumps that her failing eyes could not make out.

'You're no going to read yon letter again surely?'

'Granny –' I hesitated. Catriona had said keep it quiet, but I had to tell someone and my granny is better than most to tell things to. For one thing, she can keep a secret, better than I can. 'Gran, Catriona's getting married.'

'Married? Not to yon Alexander?'

'Yes.'

'Him with the long wavy hair and the smiling teeth?'

'Yes, yes.'

'She's a daft bit lassie then. And she's far too young to be thinking of such things.'

I was relieved. So Granny agreed with me, and on two counts: that Catriona was daft getting married at all at her age – seventeen – and that she was daft marrying Alexander. There would be at least one other person who would agree with us. Her mother.

All day, at work, I kept thinking about it. I was dying for the evening to come when I would see James and could ask him did he know, had he had a letter? I had mine with me, in the pocket of my starched apron. My mother wouldn't have recognised me if she'd come walking in to the dining room. I was all kitted out in black and white

6

looking so domestic I didn't know myself when I passed a mirror. I kept stopping, even then, after four weeks, to look closer to make sure it was me. McKinley in the service of her fellow man! And woman. It was the women who were the worst. The kids were okay. Some were sweet, and the others I glowered at behind their parents' backs. The men smiled at me, gave me big tips, didn't mind too much when I slittered a little soup on their suits; the women eyed me critically, expecting to be spattered, and they sometimes were. I wouldn't say often; just occasionally. But I knew I was not cut out for waitressing, not in the long term. I had to see the summer out because I needed the money. My trouble was I rushed too much, tried to carry too much at once. Four plates of hot meat and no tray. Asking for trouble, you might say. The manager spoke to me, naturally, said, 'Slow down, Maggie, watch what you're doing!' My other failing was that I was often talking and had my eyes on the person and not the plate of tomato soup. Tomato soup is terrible stuff for staining.

That day was even more difficult than usual. I tried as hard as I could but I just couldn't seem to keep my mind on three mushroom soups, two grilled trout, one lamb chop. . . . More than once I arrived in the kitchen to find that my mind was a complete blank except for one fact: *Catriona is getting married.* The cook got exasperated: it was a hot day, her corns were hurting, and I wasn't helping any.

I was clearing the tables after lunch when James's fair head poked round the dining-room door. I dropped my tray. Only two inches, fortunately, on to a table.

'Have you heard?' I asked. 'About Catriona?'

He nodded, and, after looking round to see that the coast was clear, came into the room. He looked very solemn. And very glum.

'Imagine Catriona getting married to *Alexander*!' I said.

'I think I'll have to go down to Edinburgh and try to stop it.'

'Stop it? But *you* can't. I mean, it's up to Catriona. She's over age.' In Scotland you can get married at sixteen without parents' consent. I suppose most people know that since Gretna Green, just over the border, is famous for runaway marriages.

'I'll have to speak to her at any rate.' He sighed. 'She's mad.'

He didn't actually go to Edinburgh but he did ring her up that evening. We both did, from a call box in a deserted spot a couple of miles from the Frasers' cottage. Catriona was very sniffy and huffy and told us to mind our own business, it was her life, etc. We took it in turns to speak, James and I, the receiver going from hand to hand. We had a big bagful of change with us so that we could talk for as long as was necessary. From Catriona's reaction, that could be next Christmas.

'Catriona, it would be a disaster,' said James.

'You're nuts,' said I.

'Alexander's not the right man for you.'

'You'd go round the twist in three months.'

'You'll ruin your life.'

'Think what a drag it would be, tied down, night and day.'

'At least wait for a while.'

'Why don't you live with him if that's what you want?'

'Be sensible, Catriona!' said James.

'Do you really fancy being a *married woman*, Catriona?' said I.

The thought struck a chill into my heart and it must have done in Catriona's too for she began to cry. I took the receiver back from James who was about to utter the next pronouncement. If I'd been at the other end I'd have hated our guts.

I told her it was all right, not to worry, not to listen to us, we were talking through holes in our heads, we didn't know anything about it, and of course it was her life, but she must understand it had been a shock getting her letter like that. She calmed off, gulped a bit and then asked what was it like up there in the glen. She sounded kind of wistful.

'It's beautiful. Gorgeous evening, all balmy and sunny and the sky's full of light still. You know the way it is up north in summer? Pity you're not here.'

'I wish I was.'

The bleeps went, James put in some more money.

'Catriona,' I said hesitantly, 'are you really so gone on Alexander?'

'Yes.' Her answer was stiff, though how could I be sure over a telephone line? Not the best medium for heart-to-hearts.

'Couldn't you come up for a couple of days?'

'No.'

She sounded sniffly again. I sighed. James made a face at me, shrugged his shoulders. I leant against a corner of the box and gazed out at the brown and purple hills. A few sheep were moving, nothing else. The world looked too peaceful to be fussed.

'Are you going to have a honeymoon?' I asked.

'No.'

I scratched my leg. Midges! Terrible things that they are, and they always seem to fancy me. Don't know why since I haven't much meat on my bones. Catriona was beginning to irritate me, in spite of the peaceful evening outside. Or maybe because of it: I wanted to be out there, a part of it.

'Catriona, what *are* you getting married for?'

Then I got it. And I felt quite idiotic for it had never even crossed my mind. In some respects – no, many – I am a simpleton. She was pregnant.

I stood and gulped air like a fish and James stared at me as if I'd gone crazy.

'Catriona is going to have a baby,' I said, putting my hand over the damp receiver.

'What?' He grabbed the clammy thing from me. 'Is it true, Catriona? Are you sure?'

I had never imagined. . . . Well, why should I? I hadn't given the relationship of Catriona and Alexander a lot of thought. I suppose, in a way, I'd written it off because I couldn't see what she saw in him. Two girls in my class at school had had to leave in the past year because they'd got pregnant and I'd felt sorry for them. They were playing the old couldn't-care-less scene but you could see in their eyes that they were frightened. Not of actually having the baby, I shouldn't think, but of what their lives were going to be like.

I took the receiver back from James. 'Listen, Catriona, you don't have to get married, you know.'

But she said she wanted to.

We ran out of money in the end and had to say goodbye. We promised we'd ring back the next evening. For a moment we stood in the box staring at one another, not knowing what to do, then we decided that what we needed was a good walk.

We took a track across the field to the hills. The sheep were bleating gently, and from somewhere, out of sight, came the lowing of cows. So tranquil. We were anything but. We were very disturbed by Catriona's news, both of us. For a while we walked in silence, heads down, watching the heather as it parted in front of us and tried to catch at our legs. It did not seem to be a time for lifting up one's eyes unto the hills.

I would hate to be pregnant. I would hate to be getting married at seventeen. Not all girls felt the same as me and many I knew were dying for the day when they found a man and settled down to have his kids and look after his house. *His* everything, because they didn't intend to do much on their own. There were still only a few who wanted careers, though my English teacher Mr Scott said that a number would change their minds after marriage. I wanted to go to university and study social anthropology and explore the world. Marriage and everything that went with it could wait. It's odd when a friend's got a problem how we start to put ourselves into the same position and judge from there. Subjective judgments are of limited use, Maggie, Mr Scott would have said, if he could have heard me thinking.

It was Catriona who was proposing to get married and have a baby, not me. So what of her? Would it suit her? It might, I conceded. Though I didn't believe it, not at all, especially when I recollected that it was Alexander she was going to marry. She had confessed to me once that he bored her, and often they didn't know what to talk about. To me, it was something of a mystery.

'They can always get divorced,' I said.

'Great!' said James.

A cock pheasant flew out from in front of us. We stopped. He had a beautiful jewel-green breast and a bright beady eye. I didn't know how people could shoot them. Whilst we watched him, we forgot Catriona.

The bird flew off low over the heather. We walked on. What was James thinking? He was indulging in a lot of frowning and pursing of lips. He strode on far too fast for me so that every now and then I had to yelp and remind him my legs were about half the size of his. He took my hand, called me 'Shorty'.

The sky was changing; the blue was ebbing, giving way

to pink and orange and palest mauve. The colours soothed me, washing away my irritation. We started to descend again. Before we reached the road, James stopped and kissed me. He put his arm round me and held me close against him. He felt warm and solid, and reliable. Someone you could depend on and lean on. If you wanted to depend and lean. What was the matter with me? I could feel the irritation building in me once more. Catriona's news had really upset me. I scratched my neck where a midge had sucked my blood.

'Perhaps it won't be so bad,' said James, stroking my hair. 'Catriona and Alexander, I mean. After all, lots of girls get married at seventeen.'

'I wouldn't say lots.' I wriggled back a little from him. 'There's the odd one.'

'Sometimes those who get married young make the best marriages.'

He sounded a bit like his grandfather when he said that. His grandfather's a lawyer and a sweet old guy but he is about fifty years older than James.

'What makes you say that?'

'Well, they can grow together.'

'Or else apart.'

'Why do you always have to be so cynical?' He released me.

'I'm realistic, that's all.'

We walked on, not holding hands now. We hadn't quarrelled, yet we were edgy with one another though we didn't really know why. Or was it because of Catriona? The change in her life seemed to be threatening us in some strange way.

Outside his parents' cottage, I took his hand.

'Mealy-mouthed McKinley!' I said. 'The big, hard-bitten cynic.'

He laughed: I was forgiven.

We went inside. We told his mother about Catriona. We had to.

Next morning, as soon as the first bands of orange were streaking the sky, Mrs Fraser set off for Edinburgh. She had not slept during the night, James told me. She drove non-stop to the salon where Catriona worked and removed her with her hands still covered in chestnut tint. They had a long devastating session during which many hurtful truths were hurled from both sides, after which both shed tears. I could hardly believe it when I got the report from Catriona. Mrs Fraser in tears! She who's always so brisk and sure of herself and having no nonsense! But then everyone can cry at times. Just as well. A good greet – Scots for cry – does you the world of good, my granny says. Not that she spends much of her time greeting. At least, I've never seen her. It would terrify me to see her in tears. To me, she's like a rock.

Mrs Fraser did her best to dissuade Catriona from marrying Alexander. She failed.

So Catriona got married.

We were all there to witness it at the Registry Office, and then afterwards, at her home, in Heriot Row, Mr and Mrs Fraser, James and I, and Grandfather Fraser, as well as Alexander's mother and father who had come over from Fife for the day. His father was a coal miner, his mother dished out the dinners at their local primary school. He said very little, reminding me of my own father; she chatted a lot telling us all about Alexander as a baby, as a schoolboy, prospective football player for Scotland, etc. He'd been good with his hands as well as his feet apparently, and used to do her hair when he was twelve years old (though he never allowed her to tell anyone), so it was no surprise when he took up hair-dressing. Alexander kept trying to shut her up, which hurt her feelings and made her sniff. She was all got up in sparkling electric blue. I admired her outfit, which cheered her up a bit. Mr Fraser was hearty, or doing his best to be; Mrs was tight-lipped and paler than I'd ever seen her. She usually has a ruddy complexion from all the outdoor exercise. Grandfather was the only one who appeared normal and undisturbed. Perhaps at his age he felt he'd seen everything. That's what my granny says. He played the charming host, poured champagne, and gave the toast to the happy couple.

The happy couple didn't radiate too much ecstasy. Alexander looked terrified. *What have I done? What's happened to me?* That was what I read in his eyes. Catriona was so white her skin looked like ivory and she had blue smudges all round her eyes, not artificial either. She wore a pink denim suit, skirt and jacket. Alexander wore a suit that was somewhere between pale grey and lilac, and didn't quite fit him, but who cared about details like that? Apart from Mrs Fraser, that is, who kept glancing at him with disbelief. Her son-in-law! I expect she was thinking that it must be a bad dream and she would waken.

When I got Catriona to myself in the bedroom for a few minutes, I asked her how she was. Truly?

'All right. A bit sick in the mornings, but the doctor says I'll get over it soon. After three months. . . .'

She went on for a bit about how you could expect to feel on top of the world after the third month and lead a normal life. *That* was not what I had meant. It was how she felt about Alexander, and marrying him, that was what I wanted to know.

'No marriage is easy. You have to work at it.'

'You're talking like a handbook,' I cried. 'Catriona, once you told me you were bored by Alexander—'

'I never did!' Her cheeks were flaring with colour. 'What a lie, Maggie!'

'You said you never knew what to say to one another.'

14

'I don't remember that.' She didn't want to. Couldn't afford to. That I realised then. 'Anyway, if I did, it was a long time ago. We've got to know each other a lot better now.'

'Obviously.'

That annoyed her. So maybe I shouldn't have made the remark. I apologised. She was as jumpy as get out, which was understandable. The biggest day of her life! I thought I'd better not say *that* aloud. I thought I'd better say as little as possible. For the deed was done, and everyone would have to make the best of it.

What thoughts to be having on someone's wedding day! It was not the most festive wedding I'd ever been at, but after a few glasses of champagne we livened up. The fizzy wine went to my head and made me giggle. Alexander's mother went all giggly too so we got on fine together and when we parted she said it had been awful nice meeting me and she hoped James and I would come across to Fife one day and visit them.

'It'll be you next, eh?' she said, elbowing my ribs.

'What do you mean?' I asked, saying each word carefully, conscious that my speech had become a trifle slurred.

'Getting hitched.'

Oh no. Oh no! I knew my eyes were rolling. I wasn't thinking about that, I informed her. I was incapable of saying the word anthropology so I stuck at social.

'You'll change your mind. They all do.' She looked fondly over at her son and his wife. His wife. Golly! 'She seems a nice lassie,' she said, with a kind of catch in her voice.

'Very nice,' I assured her.

It was the first time she had met Catriona.

Catriona and Alexander flew off to Minorca for a fortnight. Wedding present from her grandfather. One of many. He also bought them a small flat, just two rooms, bathroom and kitchen, near the Water of Leith. As he said, it would give them a start.

'Awful generous of him,' said Alexander's mother. 'I'm afraid we can't do likewise.'

'I'm sure Alexander wouldn't expect it.'

She didn't call him Alexander, though she tried. He must have asked her to. To her, he was Sandy.

We waved them off to Minorca and I flung a bag of confetti over them, emptying half of it into my own shoes. Then Catriona, like a good Scots bride, threw her bouquet. Unwittingly, I caught it. I say unwittingly because I didn't think: I saw it coming and opened my arms automatically. Of course Catriona had thrown it *at* me.

'That means it will be you next,' said Alexander's mother happily.

I thought Mrs Fraser would faint. If she had, I'm sure it would have been an all-time first.

We came back to Heriot Row from the airport and had a cup of tea; Alexander's parents departed for Fife. The house seemed quiet. I had a headache, from the champagne.

'Champagne doesn't give you a bad head,' said Mrs Fraser.

'Probably the general excitement as well,' said Mr, sliding me two aspirins.

'I can't seem to take it in,' said Mrs, who was sitting with her elbows on the kitchen table and, for once, doing nothing with her hands. 'I can't believe that Catriona is married.'

Chapter 2

And that was that, at least in the meantime. There were further developments later. But a week afterwards I'd almost forgotten the whole thing. Every now and then I'd remember, with surprise, that Catriona was married. My mind was too full of other things to think about it for long and, anyway, there wasn't much else to think about it now. All we could do was keep our fingers crossed. All I could think of was Easter Ross, and the glen of my great-great-granny in particular. Its name is Strathcarron, and the hamlet she lived in was called Greenyards.

Greenyards. For a year now, ever since my granny had told me the tale of Margaret Ross and her sister Agnes being evicted at the time of the Clearances, the name had haunted me. I wove fancies round it, dreamt about it. Sometimes, I thought it would be a fine sunny green place; at others, that it would be dark and haunted, with the blood of the Ross women which had been so brutally spilt by the sheriff's men still lying in pools on the banks of the Carron. And now, soon, I was going to find out.

'You and your ancestral home!' said James.

There would be no home there, I reminded him. The sheriff and his men had ripped off roofs, burnt the cottages. The people had had to be driven out forever so that sheep could inhabit the land and make money for the landowners.

One of my fancies was that I might find the shell of the

sisters' house and rebuild it. I could live there, grow vegetables, keep a cow and hens. Could I? Well, as I've said, it was only a fancy. But one I was rather keen on. And after all, why not? The Frasers were always talking about how marvellous it would be to have a croft and live off one's produce and get away from the strains of urban life. A notion that my family, who are dead happy with Glasgow, thank you very much, would find cracked.

I confided my idea to James. He smiled, not taking me seriously. Not that I presented it seriously; I made rather a joke of it.

'What about your anthropology?' he said.

I sighed. Difficult. The trouble is that I could do with two or three lives all running at the same time. One doesn't give you enough scope. I said so to my granny as I was packing my rucksack.

'Away ye go, lassie,' she said. 'You're aye havering. You've years in front of you. Plenty time to do all you need. You shouldne be so impatient.'

I carefully wrapped the Cairngorm brooch which had once belonged to Margaret Ross and put it in the bottom of the rucksack. It pleased me to think I was taking it back to its original home.

'Pity you can't come too, Gran.'

'I'm a bit old for the travelling now.'

She had never travelled, seemed not to have wanted to, or did not remember if she had. She watched me pack, tutted when she saw I did not put in any vests. I told her I never wore one.

'No wonder you're so peely-wally looking.'

She herself was looking pretty fit for her eighty-four years, better than she had for some time, and so I felt I was leaving her in good shape.

Mr Fraser was going to drive us part of the way to Inverness, with our bicycles strapped to the car roof, not

18

that we particularly wanted him to, but his wife insisted. She was pleased that at least we were cycling and not hitching, as we had once planned to do. That idea had upset her. My own mother had also warned me of all the dangers of hitch-hiking, and my Aunt Jessie, disaster *raconteuse par excellence*, had regaled me with numerous lurid tales of what had happened to girls who were stupid enough to accept lifts from strangers. I agreed with her, that it was a dicey thing to do, for a girl alone, but I would have James with me. 'Even so,' Aunt Jessie had said darkly, a phrase that she intended to speak volumes. Not that she ever let one phrase speak volumes: she liked details too much. Yet, in spite of the gore, she's cheery company.

So it was to be the bicycle for us! My mind boggled when I allowed myself to think about it beforehand, which I tried not to do, or I might have taken fright and not gone. The thing was that I had done scarcely any cycling before embarking on that trip; I had never owned a machine, so all of my experience had been on borrowed bikes, most of which had been too big or too small, or had brakes that didn't work or tyres that wouldn't pump up properly. Once, I had toured Glasgow on a bike looking for premises for my family's plumbing business, and that had put me off for life, or so I'd thought. It was a borrowed machine again for me: Catriona's. James had lowered the seat as far as it would go, and I'd had a few practices up and down the road outside Granny's, with Mr Farquharson waving his stick and offering advice. Balance, he cried, it was all in the balance. I didn't feel that balance came very naturally to me. Anyway, as I've said, I had decided not to think about it until I had to.

By the time my sack was packed, I was sizzling with excitement. I waltzed Granny round the room, making her laugh. She collapsed into her chair by the window,

19

saying I was an 'awfy lassie'.

'Here's the Frasers now,' she said, glancing out.

Mrs was there too, of course. She asked after Granny's health and wondered if it was wise for me to be leaving her alone? What she meant was: was it wise for me to be going away with James on my own for two whole weeks? Think of what could happen! But, after all, look what had happened to Catriona, and she had never even gone away for one night with Alexander. Mrs Fraser was confused. I could sense a battle being waged inside her head. She so much wanted to be liberal and fair. She and I can read one another quite well a lot of the time. She was full of quick nervy smiles that day, trying not to show she was bothered. Poor soul! No doubt the business over Catriona had taken it out of her, and now here was her son going off with a girl. And that girl had caught the bride's bouquet! Mrs Fraser's greatest fear was that James might marry before he graduated in medicine from Edinburgh University. So far he hadn't got the length of the door – he was starting in October – and she had grounds for worry already. Ah me!

She gave us lectures about wet socks and getting enough to eat. And we must go to a hostel every night, no sleeping rough or any of that nonsense. We'd end up with pneumonia.

'Elizabeth,' said her husband patiently, 'they're old enough to look after themselves.'

'Dinne fash yesel', Mrs Fraser,' said Granny. 'Our Maggie might seem a scatty bit lassie but underneath she's quite capable. And your Jamie's a real sensible lad.'

The sensible lad winked at me. Now I was desperate to be off. No, patience is *not* much in my line. It's one of the many things I have intentions of cultivating, sometime.

Granny hobbled out to the pavement to wave us off. She was joined by Mrs Clark, her neighbour from upstairs, and old Mr Farquharson who said mournfully that he would miss me. He certainly would, especially when it came to mealtimes and getting his washing done. Mrs Clark patted up her blue-rinsed hair and said it must be great to be young. She sighed a little but smiled at the same time, and hoped we'd have a lovely, lovely holiday. I promised her a postcard, and one to Mr Farquharson too.

'And you won't forget your old Gran?'

'How could I do that? My life wouldn't be worth living when I got back, would it?'

Everyone laughed. I kissed Granny's old cheek, hugged her hard and told her not to get up to any nonsense.

We got in to the car, Mr Fraser started the engine. We wound down the windows, waved, called out goodbye. I twisted round in my seat and waved until I could no longer see the stooped figure of my granny in her old grey skirt, flowered overall and men's laced-up boots.

James and I held hands on the back seat, and from time to time smiled at one another, like conspirators. Mrs Fraser, ricking her neck so that she was half-turned in her seat, talked to us continuously. We did not mind. We would have to listen to her for two whole weeks. We would be together without anyone interfering, or offering advice, or being anxious, or hopeful. When we were with my family in Glasgow they all gawped at James expectantly. They were always awaiting developments, such as engagement rings and marriage dates. They were wasting their time, I kept informing them, *ad nauseam*, but my mother and Aunt Jessie would always smile knowingly. They'd heard that before!

When we arrived at the point agreed on for the parting of the ways, a few miles from Inverness, Mrs Fraser said that they were going to give us lunch. Then she would know that we had a good hot meal inside us to start off with. The way she said it made it sound as if we didn't expect to eat anything for the coming fortnight. Since I am never averse to the idea of eating, I agreed without demur.

There was a nice little hotel alongside the road, with the dining room looking out on a pine forest. The windows were open, letting in the smell. It was rather nice to be served for a change, and when the waitress disappeared out of the door my mind went with her into the hot kitchen where she'd be calling out her order. Four roast lamb. . . .

Well fed, we returned to the car and James and his father unroped the bicycles from the roof rack. The moment for take-off was at hand. I leant my bicycle against the wall and strapped my rucksack on to the back carrier. It bulged out alarmingly in all directions. By the time I got on the back too, the front wheel would probably rear up into the air, like a lively horse.

'Got everything but the kitchen sink with you, eh Maggie?' said Mrs Fraser in her tinkly voice.

I made no reply, thinking it better not.

James's rucksack, of course, was more manageable. Better packed no doubt. He sat astride his bike, ready for off. I held mine propped against me, fearing I would never balance at all now, and praying that the Frasers would not actually wait to see us pedal off into the sunset.

'Come on then, Elizabeth,' said her husband, getting into the car.

She went, with more of her quick anxious smiles.

'Don't worry, mother,' James called after her.

'Goodbye. Take care!'

We waved them off. The noise of the engine died away. We were alone. For two weeks.

'Lead on, Macduff!' I cried.

22

It had to be now or never. My nerve could easily have failed me. James moved away smoothly from the kerb, I got my feet on the pedals, but not my bottom on the seat, and progressed a few yards, wobbling like crazy. I could certainly feel the weight of that sack behind me. And then, hey presto, in a flash, the stupid machine skidded out of my control, and I was flung into the ditch, where I lay, dazed and dirty, watching the front wheel spinning a couple of inches from my nose.

'Maggie, Maggie, are you all right?' James was full of concern. He picked the bicycle off me, helped me up. I hirpled over to the low stone dyke at the other side of the road and sat myself down to nurse my sores. Thank goodness my downfall had not been witnessed by Mrs Fraser! I looked at James and started to laugh.

When I had recovered from my merriment I discovered that my injuries were not serious. Only a graze on my hand, and a few bruises elsewhere. I would live, I informed him. Good, he said. He straightened out the bicycles and repacked my rucksack, taking several things out and putting them on his own bike. 'No wonder!' he kept saying. What did I have to bring all those tins with me for? There *were* shops where we were going.

It was nice sitting on the dyke in the sun. I would have been happy to spend the day there. And I was not all that delirious at the thought of mounting that nasty machine again. I closed my eyes and held my face upwards to catch the warm golden heat.

'Trouble?' asked a voice.

I opened my eyes and saw, for the first time, the two Canadian boys. I knew straightaway they were Canadian because of the little maple-leaf flags on their rucksacks, so I wasn't doing any particularly smart Conan Doyle detective work.

'Can we give you a hand?'

James refused the offer politely. I smiled at the boys. They looked nice, about the same age as James, maybe a year or so older, one with very dark hair, the other with sandy red hair and beard, and freckled face. They smiled back. Brown eyes and blue. Nice.

'Are you youth hostelling?'

'Yes,' I said.

They were too, walking and hitching from one to the other. They had been all over England and a good bit of Scotland, and now were heading for John O'Groats. They were very friendly, wanted to talk. They sat down on the wall and loosened their rucksacks from their shoulders. I took a big bar of chocolate from my pocket and broke it in four. James said no thank you, and then I realised he wasn't crazy about me hobnobbing with the boys. I shrugged. One had to be friendly to one's fellow travellers, surely.

'I'm Phil,' said the dark boy, 'and this is Mike.'

'Maggie,' I said, 'and James.'

We all said 'Hi!', even James. He did not sit down, but stood at the side of the road, arms folded across his chest, clearly wanting to be off.

'I suppose we'd better go,' I said.

'Going far?' asked Phil.

'Probably Strathpeffer,' I said. 'That's about twenty-three miles from Inverness. Isn't it, James?'

'Yes.' He didn't sound too pleased that I had divulged the information. But it was hardly Top Secret.

The boys said they never made plans, they waited to see where their lifts took them. That idea appealed to me.

I got up and lifted my bike. Now I was going to have to ride off under the eyes of these two boys! And retain my dignity if possible. I gave myself a little talk. There's nothing to it, riding a bicycle's as easy as falling. . . . Yes well. . . . You can do it, McKinley! *You have to*. I had, after all, ridden bicycles before, if only after a fashion, and unladen.

I got my bottom up on to the seat first this time, kept my foot against the dyke to steady me, took a deep breath and went whizzing off, no bother at all.

''Bye,' called the boys.

'Goodbye,' I called, not daring to look back, or lift my hand to wave.

'It was that stupid rucksack to blame,' said James, catching up with me easily.

'They were nice. The boys.'

'They were all right.'

We pedalled in silence most of the way to Inverness. I needed all my breath for the effort. I did not know what James needed his for, he could have cycled non-stop through the day without puffing. Was he jealous? The idea infuriated me. Did he think he owned me? I glanced sideways at him – only for a split second since I was on the verge of wobbling – and saw he looked kind of brooding. He could be moody at times. So could I of course, and maybe I wouldn't have liked him chatting up a couple of girls, offering them chocolate and so forth. He'd get over it, and there was no point in having a row in the first half-hour of being on the road.

We went through Inverness, avoiding the busiest parts. The traffic made me jumpy, and once or twice I took to the pavement and pushed the bike along the gutter.

A mile or so outside the town, we were passed by an open-tailed lorry carrying Mike and Phil. They were sitting on a pile of empty sacks at the back. They waved and yelled to us. We waved back, I at my peril, and then they were gone, around the bend of the road. I couldn't help wishing we were hitching; it looked an awful lot easier and faster. At this rate they'd be at John O'Groats before we even got to Beauly, which was only about fourteen miles away. Only!

'It's nice being away on our own like this, isn't it?' said James.

I nodded. It was, very nice. We smiled at one another, and I wobbled again. I was all right as long as I was concentrating on the bicycle and nothing else. I couldn't even look much at the scenery which was very attractive, especially when the road was running close to the Beauly Firth. James pointed out the Black Isle to me beyond, so-called because of its rich black soil. The road was fairly flat here at least: that was always something.

When we had done about half the distance to Beauly, according to James, he said that we would stop for a little rest and a drink round the next bend.

Round the next bend we found Phil and Mike sitting by the side of the road. Well, fancy that! They greeted us like old friends now. I was careful to greet them with a little less enthusiasm, mindful of James's feelings, but he himself was warmer to them this time, no doubt regretting having been a bit sullen before, for he's naturally good-mannered.

We dismounted, joined them on the grass verge. James unpacked our bottle of coke and offered them some, they offered us a share of their biscuits. We munched and drank and they told us about some of the lifts they'd had and the people they'd met. Mike was really funny and good at imitating people's accents. He could do Cockney and then switch to Liverpudlian. I told him his Scots was a bit off the beam and coached him a little. He managed to say, 'It's a braw bricht moonlicht nicht the nicht', which made Phil laugh his 'heid aff'. We all had a good laugh. After half an hour, James suggested it was time we were moving off.

'See you again, no doubt,' said Phil.

We saw them again about ten minutes later. Round the

26

next bend but one. I had a puncture, or rather, Catriona's back tyre did, so I couldn't really be held to blame for that. And no sooner had we got off than the Canadian boys appeared, walking.

'We seem to be fated to bump into each other,' said Phil.

'It's like that on the road,' said Mike.

'Yes, that's one of the things I like about it,' said Phil. 'Say, can we give you a hand, James?'

But James did not need a hand, so the three of us sat on the grass and enjoyed the sun whilst he sorted the tube. I wouldn't have had the foggiest inkling as to what to do, needless to say. He put the wheel back on, wiped his hands.

We said goodbye again.

'At this rate we won't get very far today,' said James.

'It doesn't matter, does it?'

I felt released from all idea of time. It was a marvellously exhilarating feeling. Freedom. Heady stuff. Even if only for a fortnight.

A few minutes later we had to draw in to the side as we heard a lorry approaching. It slowed down and drew up just in front of us. The Canadian boys were standing in the back, waving.

'Come on,' cried Phil. 'Want a lift? We can put your bikes on the back.'

I knew that James would not want the lift, he has ideas about purity and consistency, like sticking to things once you've started, which I don't have to the same degree, but I couldn't resist the thought of covering a few miles without having to push those pedals round. My calves were aching. I said that'd be great. I let Phil and Mike lift my bike on to the back of the lorry and pull me up. James swung his own bike up without a word, and clambered aboard.

'All set?' called out the driver.

'All set,' called back Phil.

Now I could enjoy the scenery. It seemed to me a marvellous way to travel, seated up high on the back of a truck, with someone else doing the work. The lorry was going to Beauly.

'A few more lifts and we could be in Strathcarron tonight,' I shouted to James over the sound of the diesel exhaust.

Either he didn't hear me, or didn't wish to, but he did not turn his head.

Chapter 3

We did not get to Strathcarron that night, we stayed at Strathpeffer as planned. And so did the Canadian boys.

The lorry dropped us off in the town square at Beauly. It was a square with a road going through the middle and on either side were shops, hotels and cafés. The cafés, promising refreshment, drew my eyes, but I did not dare say I was hungry to James. Hadn't we had a three-course meal just two or three hours ago? I was pleased therefore when Mike said his throat was dried up by all that gunk from the lorry fumes and he could use a cup of coffee.

'Me too,' I said.

'I wouldn't mind a sandwich either,' said Phil.

'Neither would I,' I said.

'Maggie's always hungry,' said James.

We dragged all our clobber across to a café and had coffee and toasted sandwiches, then more coffee and apple pie. It wasn't bad but it cost a bomb, compared with what it would have done in Glasgow. James said they had to make a living during the summer, there wasn't much going for them during the winter. The way he said it it sounded as if he was sort of ticking me off. He was edgy of course, on account of the company. I knew things weren't working out as he'd planned but it was only the first day after all. Part of me felt sorry for him. And the other part? Well, I have to admit I was enjoying myself. I was torn. Common dilemma for me to be in.

'They've got the oil all year round now though,' I said. We had seen two lorries going by whilst we were sitting there, laden with pipes, heading presumably for Invergordon and Nigg Bay.

We had a wee chat about the North Sea Oil, Mike and Phil asking us how we felt about it.

'It's bound to change Scotland,' said Phil. 'Do you think it'll spoil all your lovely countryside?'

'Not all,' I said. 'It's only in certain areas.'

James came to life. It was a subject he felt strongly about. The discovery of oil was a blight on our nation, it would change the country, the people, everything! We would be exploited; it would not be us who would become rich. He wanted Scotland left as it was. Look at the Cromarty Firth, its beauty spoiled by oil rigs, platforms, and pipelines!

I sighed. I agreed with him on most points but felt it wasn't all that simple. It was all right for James with his Georgian house in Edinburgh and a cottage in Inverness-shire wanting Scotland left unmarked so that he could enjoy tramping through its lonely beautiful glens.

'If the glens could be repopulated. . . .' I was thinking of my great-great-granny's glen.

'The glens won't be, Maggie. They'll suck what they need from the sea, destroy the coastline and when they're finished, abandon the lot and we'll be left with a derelict mess.'

We sat for a moment gloomily contemplating the prospect. Progress! What a pain in the neck it is at times. But was this progress?

'Anyway, there's much of Scotland that will never be touched,' I said. 'It's too remote, and nobody would be interested.'

'That's true,' said James, cheering up a bit.

'My great-great-granny's glen will probably stay the

30

same. At least, it looks as if it would from the map.'

'Where's that?' asked Phil.

'Strathcarron.'

'For goodness' sake! I want to go there myself. My great-great-grandfather was evicted from Glencalvie during the Clearances. That's further up the glen.'

'My great-great-granny was cleared from Green-yards!' I turned to James. 'Isn't that amazing?'

'Oh I don't know! Hundreds of thousands of people were evicted during the Clearances and they must have a lot of descendants by this time.'

'But to think of Phil coming all the way from Canada—'

'Most of those who were evicted went to Canada or Australia. I suppose quite a number must take the pilgrimage back every year to the home of their ancestors.'

I could have bared my teeth at him. I hate it when he puts on his pompous manner. In spite of statistics, I was impressed at meeting Phil who had come from Canada to Easter Ross to find the home of his ancestors, and met me coming from Glasgow to find the home of mine.

'My surname's Ross as a matter of fact,' said Phil.

'Really?' I whooped. 'My great-great-granny was a Ross.'

'Maggie,' said James, 'nearly all the inhabitants of the glen were Rosses. In those days most of Easter and Wester Ross was inhabited by Rosses.'

'Nevertheless. . . .'

'Maybe you and I are related, Maggie,' said Phil.

'Could be.'

'Half of Scotland is related if you go back far enough,' said James.

'Let's have some more coffee,' said Mike.

'Yes, please,' I said.

'No, thanks,' said James, 'not for me. We ought to be going, Maggie. We've still a few miles to cover and we want to be sure of getting in to the hostel. At this time of year they fill up quickly.'

I felt exhausted and incapable of pushing on anywhere, except perhaps ten yards up the road. My legs were still aching and a couple of bruises were coming up nicely on my arms. I wished there was a hostel in Beauly, but there wasn't. So, Strathpeffer it must be.

'Think we should make for there too, Mike,' said Phil. 'If we go on to the next one we might be late and not get in.'

The next one was Carbisdale Castle, close to Strathcarron, and tomorrow we would be there. With a bit of luck! Like a lift or two?

We said cheerio to the boys, see you later, and pedalled off. I had high hopes that they would appear shortly in a lorry that would be amenable to lifting two more weary travellers plus bikes, but when they did pass us it was in the back of a smoothly purring Jaguar. They waved.

'That's the way to travel,' I said.

'Nonsense! You see the countryside better this way. And smell all the scents.'

He was right. And the countryside looked beautiful with the late-afternoon sun flooding across it. There was time to notice the cows, the changing colours of the hills, and spot wild flowers growing in the hedgerows. I even forgot my aching limbs and managed to fall off only once. And that was because I was craning my neck to see a purple flower and swerved into the ditch.

We came to a sign saying *Strathpeffer 6*.

'Only six more miles, Maggie! You're doing fine.'

The last six felt like sixty. James said that by tomorrow I would feel broken in and it wouldn't seem nearly so arduous. I said I'd wait and see, and I was right to be sceptical.

Strathpeffer is a spa town, rather pretty, with hills ringing it. There were lots of big houses and hotels and a spa pavilion. The hostel itself had once been a large private residence, built in Victorian times. It sat up on a hill overlooking the valley, and was now covered with greyish-green harling, with salmon-painted window surrounds and a white door. Phil and Mike were sitting on the front lawn.

'There's room for you,' said Mike. 'We booked you in.'

We saw the warden, handed in our membership cards, and then James went off with Mike and Phil whilst I went up to find a bunk in a girls' dormitory. I washed my face and combed my hair, and brushed my jeans off with my hand. Then I put a little bit of colour on my eyes, just to give myself a boost.

The three of them were in the kitchen cooking when I got there. The Canadian boys were heating up tinned hamburgers, James was cooking spaghetti and heating up a sauce of meat, tomato and mushrooms, that his mother had prepared and given us. It smelled and looked great.

'You're well organised,' said Mike, eyeing our meal.

I felt I should have offered them some, but how could I? There was more than enough but it was James's mother's sauce. His brow was furrowed under his overhanging lock of fair hair, as he stood by the cooker stirring the pot.

We all ate at the same table; we couldn't have done anything else. James did not say much, Phil and Mike chatted freely. They were both university students in Ottawa, about to go into their third years. I knew that would make James feel a bit at a disadvantage because he'd just left school. Mike was studying physics, Phil geology. He said that Scotland was very interesting for a geologist and he hoped to come back sometime and do research work. James made no comment, but continued winding his spaghetti around his fork. I told the boys that I wanted to study social anthropology.

'You could come to Canada and study Indian and Eskimo settlements,' said Phil. 'That would be interesting. Eskimo life is fascinating.' He'd spent a summer up north, in Canada; he told us something about it.

James pushed his plate away. He said he must have eaten too many sandwiches, he wasn't hungry. He wanted to go for a walk.

We went after we'd cleared up. Without our Canadian friends. I had known for the last two or three hours that we were building for a row and that the sooner we had it the better. It's like waiting for a thunderstorm to break. In the end, I could wait no longer and had to invoke it myself.

'What's the matter with you? You've got a face like a sour lemon on you!'

That did it. I got the full blast. I was selfish and thoughtless, I only did what I wanted, and he had to fall in with me. I was encouraging the Canadian boys. No: I was flirting with them.

I denied it all hotly. Very hotly. I could feel my cheeks flaming, my eyes blazing. I was only being friendly to strangers in a strange land. Anyway, I did not belong exclusively to him.

But I was his steady girl friend, he countered; at least, he had thought so. Was I?

'Yes. But that doesn't mean I can't *talk* to any other boys.'

Well no, he would agree with that, but this was different. We were spending our holiday with two other boys, instead of being together, on our own, as we had planned, and wanted it.

34

'You're exaggerating everything, James! We've spent part of today—'

'If it was left to you we'd spend the next two weeks with them. We'd end by trailing up Strathcarron in a jolly band looking for the homes of our ancestors!'

Couldn't I see his point of view? he asked. He had been looking forward to this trip so much, he didn't want it spoiled, and yet here we were quarrelling, on the first day. And why? Because of Phil and Mike.

I sighed. Of course I saw his point of view. And he was sweet and nice and he did care for me. I liked him pretty well too, I reminded myself, so I mustn't spoil it either. The trouble is I like excitement, and often that can be dangerous and lead to disruption. I know it full well, from experience. Keep the heid, McKinley! James is a good lad. I could imagine my granny's voice cautioning me.

We made it up. I told him I was sorry, I had not meant to upset him, did not want to, and of course I preferred his company to the boys. We were going to have a fantastic holiday and nothing would be allowed to spoil it. A light shower of summer evening rain sent us running for cover under a birch tree. We stood, arms around one another, leaning against the silver-grey trunk, gazing at one another with mooney smiles. He *was* nice. He kissed me, gathering me close to him. We clung to one another like the last two souls left on a planet, feeling we might have lost one another, aware of the possibility. There was always that possibility. I shivered.

The rain rattled gently on the leaves, making them shiver and shake, and some silver drops of water trembled for a second on the edges of the green spikes before sliding down to alight on our faces. I felt bewitched by the evening. It was full of light and gentle movement, and, from somewhere high above, came the trilling of birds. The mountains stretching northwards were an incredible misty purplish-blue colour. I could have written a poem that even Mr Scott my English teacher might not have scorned. I felt poetic and romantic. You, Maggie McKinley! Yes, I, Maggie McKinley: that was how I felt.

So I suppose that when James told me he loved me it was not surprising that I said I loved him too. I had never said it before, had never even wanted to think about it, had done my best to avoid the question.

'Do you mean it? Really?'

I nodded, not trusting myself to speak. But let it be, James, that's enough at present, I wanted to say, but somehow could not without dampening that look on his face. I did not want him to push it further, to get more intense. He was pretty intense as it was: his eyes were just about eating me up, and yet, oddly, at the same time, had a kind of glazed look that made me feel he didn't really see me at all. This was a different James: a stranger. No, not that really, but his familiarity was blurred by that look on his face which I had never seen before.

He pulled me closer to him. Again, he told me that he loved me, more than anything else in the world. 'You must believe me, Maggie, you must!' I did believe him, but I couldn't cope with any more emotion. A little bit at a time is enough for me. That goes for sex too. It was another thing I couldn't cope with, wasn't ready for, and didn't see why I should be, in spite of all those girls in my class claiming such vast sexual experience. There were plenty of others, like me, not wanting to get there yet. At that moment I felt on the brink. I panicked. I pushed James away. He blinked.

'See, it's stopped raining!' I pointed outwards, and his eyes followed my finger as if mesmerised. Then I shook the tree raining us with drops of water like confetti. Confetti!

'Yes,' said James, who sounded as stunned as he

36

looked. I felt so sorry for him, wanted to put my arms round him again, but couldn't, for that would have returned us to where we had been a moment before. I had had to push him away. But how could I tell him that? I didn't seem to be able to anyway. Maybe I should have tried.

I stepped out on to open ground, tilting my face back. Only a few spots of water touched it. Thinking of confetti reminded me of Catriona. I asked James if they'd had any word from Minorca.

'We had a postcard yesterday, didn't Mother tell you? They just said they were having a lovely time, weather was perfect, etc.' He came to take my hand. He had changed back into my more familiar James.

I took his hand and led him on to the path. Everything looked fresh and green and glistening. How beautiful the world was! It made me catch my breath.

'It might be quite nice to be married, don't you think?' said James.

'In middle-age, yes, why not?'

'Maggie!'

'Come on, let's run, I feel like running.'

My legs had ceased to ache from their earlier efforts, they moved smoothly beneath me, as if winged. I needed action.

We returned to the hostel as the evening was cooling. There was still a lot of light left, and there would be almost until midnight. There was a sing-song going on in the common room. I kept hold of James's hand as we went in. Phil and Mike, who were there, waved to us, beckoning us over.

'Yes, let's join them,' said James easily.

The boys were sitting with two Australian girls, Betty and Prue. We were introduced. We sat on the floor and joined in the singing, and James kept his arm loosely around my shoulders. It was nice being there, as a part of the crowd, all singing together, laughing and talking. I liked the feeling of being amongst people from all over the world. More than ever it made me want to travel, see new places, meet new people. Would James? He might, if it was to go with me.

At eleven, it was bed-time. I could have stayed up all night. I'm a real night bird, dead useless at the early morning scene. I said good-night to James, Phil and Mike and trundled off to the girls' dormitory. Betty and Prue were in the bunks next door to me so we had a good long yak about all sorts of things and they said if I ever got to Australia, which I had every intention of doing sometime, I was to look them up. The girl in the bunk below me kept saying, 'Do you mind?' so we had to give over, though I kept thinking of things I wanted to ask them.

'Have you ever been to the Central Desert?' I whispered.

'What?' asked Prue.

'Do you mind?' asked the girl below me.

I found it difficult to sleep. Everyone else in the dormitory seemed to be finding it only too easy, judging from the snores and whistles and grunts, but I was as wide awake as the traditional sparrow at dawn. There was much on my mind. I kept thinking of standing with James beneath the silver birch in the rain. I thought of Catriona and Alexander. I thought of my granny. My mind would not rest. I began to count sheep louping the burn in the glen down below the cottage where my granny used to live.

The next thing I knew it was morning and everyone in the dormitory was up but me. Betty and Prue's beds were all neatly folded up, and my bunk-mate was standing in front of the mirror teasing her hair into a bush to stand out around her head. After that she applied elaborate make-up with such care and concentration that she did not even blink or look round when I sat up. I didn't know where she thought she was going up here. And on such a day. For I could hear what kind of day it was. It was blowing a gale out there, rattling the window frames, flaying the panes with rain. I snuggled back down into my sleeping bag, not much fancying the idea of cycling in the teeth of that. Surely James would not expect to. Eternal optimist McKinley!

A male cough at the doorway made the girl turn her head. James said, 'I'm sorry to disturb you but I'm looking for my friend Maggie.'

Friend Maggie put up her head and said, 'Here!'

'Aren't you getting up yet, you lazy thing?'

'Just coming.'

He went away, I took five minutes more, then thought I'd better crawl out and see how the world was doing.

We were last in the kitchen making breakfast. In fact, James had cooked it by the time I arrived so we sat down straightaway to sausages and fried eggs. I apologised for being so late.

'It's all right.' He was full of smiles. 'Phil and Mike asked me to say goodbye to you, by the way.'

'Oh, have they gone?'

'About half an hour ago.'

'Betty and Prue too?'

'They went with them.'

I cursed myself for not having been up earlier. My slothful habits had got the better of me on many an occasion in the past.

'You should have called me. I'd have liked to have said goodbye to them.'

James shrugged. 'Doesn't matter, does it? After all, it's like that on the road, you meet people one day and they're gone the next.'

That annoyed me because I felt that was the way James wanted it, whereas I like making new friends, and keeping them. Still, how could I have hoped to keep Betty and Prue from Australia and Phil and Mike from Canada?

We did our chores, recovered our cards, and got ready to leave. James said I would need my oilskins on – understatement that – or rather, Catriona's oilskins. They were miles too big and cumbersome for me. I felt like a yellow baby elephant cavorting about in the lobby of the hostel. Outside was a blanket of wet greyness, topped by a grey sky that you knew wouldn't have the slightest chance of letting even a sliver of blue in during the course of the day. Not a sign of the mountains! There was no point in waiting for the rain to pass over or any of that nonsense. It must be faced.

It seemed to be coming straight from the north. We had to cycle, one behind the other, with our heads down, and every time a car or lorry passed we were sprayed up to the knees with water. What a crazy way to spend a holiday! I thought of Catriona sunning herself on the beach in Minorca. Lucky thing! Then I thought of Catriona in her delicate condition, with Alexander on the beach in Minorca, and did not envy her. I still preferred to be me in my soaking state, slogging it out against the wind and rain on a road in Easter Ross. I sang to myself under my breath to keep my spirits up. There was no such thing as conversation on this journey. All I saw was the back view of James leading the way, except when we stopped for cups of coffee, which we did fairly often. I had to, or I'd never have survived.

The second half of the journey was really tough going, after we left the Cromarty Firth and cut across the hills to the Dornoch Firth. The road twisted and turned, up hill and down dale. Many of the braes were so steep that we had to get off and push the bikes, which wasn't much of a picnic since the bikes were laden up and we were sweating under oilskins. We came to one long stretch of bleak moorland, dun-coloured, and so desolate looking that all I could think of was being on some unpopulated planet. And wanting to get off fast. As luck would have it, the rain increased here, becoming quite torrential. There was no cover anywhere: not a tree, not a shepherd's hut. There were no sheep up here even. Only us.

We cycled on, and when we couldn't cycle, we walked.

'An inn,' I spluttered, hardly able to believe it. Ahead was a white building. I thought it might be a mirage and didn't believe it until we were upon it.

Altnamain Inn. A welcome rest for travellers right enough. We rested there for an hour and partook of a little refreshment.

'On!' said James. 'We have to get to Carbisdale.'

Once the road started to descend the countryside softened, trees reappeared, and sheep, and the odd cottage. We stopped to look down on the rain-lashed waters of the Dornoch Firth. It was a fine sight, and it meant we were getting closer.

The run down to the firth was great, I could free-wheel and let my legs dangle. Speed at last after all that snail-crawling against the wind! I almost freaked out. Trees fringed the water's edge, and through them we glimpsed the grey-blue waters tipped with white. At Ardgay, just before you come to the Sutherland border, we turned off again into the hills. The last lap. That was what it felt like.

Then we came to a signpost saying *Greenyards 5*. I jumped off my bicycle.

'It exists, James!'

He laughed. 'We have to take the other road now. But tomorrow we'll come back and go that-a-way!'

Chapter 4

Carbisdale Castle is a huge stone pile standing on a spur overlooking the Shin Valley and half of Sutherland. That was deliberate. We heard why later, and the story made me chuckle.

The castle was built around 1903 for the Dowager Duchess of Sutherland who had had a bit of a dispute with her in-laws. She had been the ex-Duke's third wife and it seems that the Sutherlands were not too fond of her, for one reason and another. After her husband died they said she was taking away things from Dunrobin Castle – their main seat – that she had no right to. I've often heard the same kind of tales back home in Glasgow: everybody in a tizzy about who should get what after someone dies. Anyway, she burned some documents that she shouldn't have and had to spend six weeks in Holloway! As a privileged prisoner though, with her maid in attendance and special food brought in. When she came out, the Sutherlands thought she should have a castle suitable for a Dowager Duchess but they made one condition: it must not be in Sutherland. So she built it on the extreme edge of Easter Ross looking right over the Sutherland lands and straight down on to their private railway line. She sat up in her castle and watched them passing in their private train. They retaliated by putting blinds on all the carriage windows. And the servants were forbidden even to keek round the blinds. Must have been quite a temptation, one I might not have been able to resist. What a way for grown folk to get on!

We went up a long drive through gorgeous well-wooded grounds, not particularly well kept up, but that's the way I like gardens to be. I hate them when they're manicured. There was even an old abandoned tennis court. Forty-love to the Duchess! We passed a building which might have been servants' quarters formerly but now said *private*, then a sweep round, and we came to the courtyard with a stone wall running round it. The castle was enormous!

'Are we really going to stay here?' I felt quite impressed.

There was a clock tower with clocks on three faces. None on the fourth, the one that faced out over Sutherland. Apparently, the Duchess wouldn't give the Sutherlands the time of day! So it's said.

We went at once to the wall to look down at the view, and as we reached it, out came the sun, momentarily. My chin only came to the top of the parapet so I had to climb up to get a decent look. I saw the River Shin curving below us, hills beyond, trees, cottages and small dots in the fields that must have been sheep.

'Shall we go in?' said James, after a few minutes. 'And get all these wet clothes off!'

We went in, and the first person we encountered was Phil Ross.

'Hi! We were wondering if you'd make it here today.'

The boys had been here for hours: they'd been dead lucky with lifts.

'Are Betty and Prue with you?'

'They pushed on, they wanted to get to John O'Groats tonight. They've only got two or three days left in Scotland.'

A pity. Apart from anything else, it might have

43

softened James for the girls would have evened the numbers and made him less inclined to worry that either Phil or Mike might be paying too much attention to me. It was all rather silly that I had to bother about such things and it irritated me. I longed for the simple life. I often do. Never seem to get it though.

We checked in and had a look round the castle. The walls of the corridors had been painted a nice coral colour which made the place look bright and gay. Most of the rooms were big and still quite gracious, especially the two sculpture galleries, one upstairs and one down. It was amazing to see all the stuff that had been left when the castle had been given to the hostels association by its last owner. White marble statues on pedestals, a wild marble mantlepiece signed by its maker, a professor from Florence, and lots of paintings. The staircase was of dark wood, heavily carved, and had huge round knobs all the way up. They amused me. They were about ten inches or so in diameter and made of fruit, apples, strawberries, bananas and the like, all in wood. Crazy!

The boys were all in dormitory ten. It used to be known as the Spook Room, the warden told us. Well, of course a castle like that would have a ghost. And who else would that be but the Duchess herself? She had been sighted on several occasions. She appeared to favour a white satin gown for her haunting and she liked going up and down the staircase. I wondered if she touched those knobs as she came down. And some hostellers at different times had reported seeing another ghost, that of a little girl in a long dress with pantaloons showing at the bottom. She had been dancing through the corridors and singing.

'They might come and visit you tonight,' I said to the boys. 'When I see you in the morning your hair'll be standing on end!'

None of them believed in ghosts of course. Did I? My

immediate reaction is disbelief always, and then I start to wonder. How can you be certain? Surely it's an area for doubt.

'There are more things in heaven and earth,' said I, airily.

'You sit on the stairs all night, Maggie,' said Phil, 'and maybe you'll see the Duchess pass by.'

'She'd probably walk over me! Or through me.'

It was a tempting thought, to sit out a night vigil, but I didn't think the warden would go for it. Lights out at eleven, and everybody in bed!

James and I cooked our supper together. Bangers and beans. I was starved and could have eaten the pot as well. James had that serious look on his face again as he stood with a fork suspended over the sizzling golden sausages. You'd have thought he was preparing something *cordon bleu* for the Queen herself. His forehead looked like corrugated cardboard.

'Relax,' I said, then decided to take the bull by the horns. I can't tread lightly round a situation in any case. 'You've no need to be jealous, I've told you. I'm not going to run off into the night with Phil and Mike. Too wet out there anyway.'

'I'm not jealous.' He turned a sausage vehemently, splattering his wrist with hot fat which he disdained to wipe off, and so an angry patch flared up there later to remind us of our little spat. 'Why should I be jealous?'

'Dear knows! Honestly, James, you are so stupid at times!' I might have marched off, if I'd had my sausages inside me already. It's amazing how something so unedifying as hunger acts as a brake on the higher emotions. My tummy was rumbling and the smell was really getting to me. I couldn't take my eyes off the food. I have a one-track mind, my mother often says, and my sister Jean, who is inclined to be plump, says it isn't fair that I should be able to eat so much and remain so skinny.

James turned the sausages over again, even though they didn't need it. I watched them, mesmerised, as they spat and hissed. It was as if they were expressing James's anger. What was the matter with us? Was there anything? Probably not, I decided, it was just that we were suddenly alone together after always having been with his parents or mine, or my granny, or Catriona. We'd kept thinking it would be marvellous to be alone but now that we were we didn't seem to be able to cope with it.

'Come on, James, let's eat,' I said, in a peace-offering tone of voice. 'You're tormenting me. You like to, don't you?' I made a face at him.

'No, not really. Well . . . . perhaps just a little bit. Sometimes you ask for it.' He grinned, and was all right again. A little cloud had passed over the sun, you might say.

Half-way through our meal, we were joined by the Canadians. James struggled hard to be welcoming, and was. I could see that the battle raging inside him was pretty fierce and didn't quite understand why, for the boys weren't much of a threat to him.

Phil had an Ordnance Survey map of the area with him which he spread out on the table when we'd finished eating.

'See this, Maggie.' His finger traced a line. 'That's Strathcarron. And here is Wester Gruinards. That must be Greenyards!'

'It's the Gaelic for it,' said James.

'And if we go a little bit further we come to Croick. That's the church where my great-great-grandpa sheltered in the churchyard, and then further into the hills is Glencalvie where he came from.'

'Where did your folks come from?' Mike asked James.

'Mine seemed to come out of thin air. Gezingo! First you

don't see them – then you do. They haven't got any history.' He shook his head mock-mournfully. He was really a cheerful boy, always making jokes and larking about.

'Your folks got a history, James?' asked Phil.

'I don't know,' said James off-handedly, though I'm sure he did, with his family for a background. 'Somewhere in the Highlands probably.'

Phil studied the map again. 'We thought we'd go up to Strathcarron tomorrow.'

'*We*?' said Mike. 'I like the plans he has for me. Tell you what, why don't you and Maggie go in pursuit of old glory and James and I'll go bird-watching? I believe there are some fabulous birds out in the Dornoch Firth.'

I didn't think it was a serious suggestion but for a second both James and Phil looked as if they did, and I thought that Phil was about to say okay, so I jumped in hurriedly and suggested that we all went to Strathcarron. We could take a picnic. Then I realised that it would have been better if I'd kept my mouth shut. Big mouth McKinley!

'How would we all get there?' said James.

'We could double up on the bikes. "Daisy, Daisy, give me your answer do", sang Mike. '"I'm half crazy. . ."'

'You don't have to tell us,' said Phil.

'Do you have that song in Canada too?' I asked.

'Sure thing,' said Mike. '"It won't be a stylish marriage. . ."'

Phil, who had been looking at James, said, 'Mike and I can go on our big flat feet. Don't worry about us.'

'Perhaps we'd better wait and see what the weather's like in the morning,' said James. 'If it's like this we'd all get drenched.'

We left it at that.

I had to go and make a phone call to Glasgow. I liked to

check in regularly and find out what everybody was up to. Besides, I was a wee bit worried about my mother who had sounded low the last time I spoke to her. Her 'nerves' were playing her up again and she had been lamenting that she could have done with me at home, was it not about time I came back to see my family, I did have a family, or had I forgotten? How could you forget a family like mine? But where they are concerned you have to be tough so I had gritted my teeth and told my mother that I'd be home when I'd said and not before. They would survive. James said that my family relies on me too much.

There was a phone in the hostel. My father answered, and straight away, without any niceties like how are you, he launched into a great saga about the tribulations of McKinley and Campbell, Plumbing Engineers. There are always tribulations in our business, and whenever there are triumphs they are not dwelt on. According to my father, we were on the verge of bankruptcy. Again!

'Your Uncle Tam and I are fair worried,' he added.

My father's great at making statements like that. A bit unnecessary after what had gone before.

'Come on, Dad, things aren't that bad.'

But how should I know since I wasn't even there? I was gallivanting all over the place spending money.

'My own,' I snapped, my patience ready to go like over-stretched elastic. 'I earned it.' Carrying hot plates of tomato soup and lamb chops, and even worse, taking away the empties. Other people's mess doesn't exactly turn me on.

'Aye, and I have to earn money to keep you at the school.'

I groaned. Not all that again! I couldn't bear it. I asked to speak to my mother. She wasn't much more cheerful and I had to listen to the bit about the business again, though in less detail. She was fed up because my dad had said they couldn't afford a holiday this year, when she'd been hoping to go to Morecambe. Last year they'd gone to Scarborough, and what a lovely time they'd had. I put more money into the box and made a face at the wall. If there was one thing I must make sure of in my life it was that I didn't end up moaning and groaning like my mother at her age. Of course, as she had often told me herself, I had the ball at my feet and the world was open. The ball had never been at her feet and I had to remember that.

'Look, Mum, why don't you and Aunt Jessie go to Blackpool for a weekend? I'm sure you could afford that.'

She wasn't though. Aunt Jessie happened to be there and was hoping to have a word with me. She came on the line.

'How are you, hen? And how's James?' Her voice was all soft and gooey.

'Fine. Sends you his love.' That would please her.

Aunt Jessie gushed and sighed about James, lovely laddie and all that (how folk repeat themselves!), wasn't I lucky and so forth. If I had to marry James, my family wouldn't be all that put out. They'd say, 'Och well, these things happen,' and the next thing you'd know would be that my mother and Aunt Jessie would be sitting in the shop knitting white bootees and discussing names. My father would be less pleased, but he'd calm off after a good talking-to by my mother.

I switched the subject from James to Blackpool. Aunt Jessie said that was a good idea and she'd work on my father and uncle about it. Then she dropped her voice to say my mother could be doing with a break, she was kind of twitchy at the moment.

'She'd like fine to have you home, Maggie. But I don't think you should come. You've your own life to lead.'

Referring to my life, she was thinking primarily of

49

James, not of the pursuit of my career. If I was to be awarded the Nobel Peace Prize my family would be less impressed than if I was to walk up the aisle of St Giles Cathedral in Edinburgh on the arm of James Fraser.

Sister Jean came on next. With a lot of giggles, and remarks off-stage from her friend Lorraine, she told me she was going steady with a boy who lived along the road. A pimply glaecid-looking youth. I didn't say so, though no doubt I might at some future date when she was annoying me. For a moment I felt homesick and wished I was there with them all in the wee flat above the shop, in spite of the moans and groans and my mother's nerve trouble. Then I thought of the hills and rivers out there and the smell of pines, and of James patiently waiting for me, and the moment passed.

Another quick word with my mother, with everyone yelling cheerio in the background, and I replaced the receiver. James was leaning against the wall. He suggested a walk; I agreed.

The rain had stopped but the evening was overcast and had nothing of the sparkling quality of the night before. Not that I minded. It was a different mood, that's all.

'What did you have to get us tied up with Phil and Mike for tomorrow?' said James.

'We don't have to go with them. Not if you don't want to.'

'How can we avoid it now? We'd have to be downright rude.'

That is something James would never be. I am more capable of it. Much more. Not that I consider *that* to be a virtue. But it happens sometimes when I forget myself and my temper loops the loop.

The evening might not have been bright but the smells were delicious, a blend of pine and damp undergrowth. The hedgerows were full of stuff: all kinds of grasses that I couldn't resist plucking to make a feathery bouquet – some were pink – and then there were dog roses, blackberries, ferns, vetches, foxgloves. We passed a honeysuckle bush whose scent was so strong and heady that James had to drag me away eventually for I could have stood there in a dream just inhaling it. Hooked on honeysuckle. The idea appealed to me.

We idled along, stopping to look at the river, talking, finding new flowers in the undergrowth which James was able to identify and name. And every now and then we stopped to kiss one another. We were contented. Looking back on the holiday, that seems to have been the best evening we had. We were very much in harmony with one another, we let all issues lie, we avoided anything that might have marred the peace. It was so quiet too with the mist hanging in the trees, narrowing our world down to a stretch of road and a glimpse of moor or river on either side. We met no one.

'I feel as if I'm really up north,' said James. 'It's a kind of "away" feeling.'

I nodded.

This felt different from our glen in Inverness-shire. Easter Ross is hilly rather than mountainous, less dramatic, more forested, softer. Lower-keyed, said James, hitting it on the head. It had its own appeal. The mountains in Wester Ross are very dramatic, said James, who knew most of Scotland well, each one standing out clearly and with a very distinctive shape. He was going to take me there on this trip. But we never made it. We planned to go up to John O'Groats too. We didn't make that either.

The mist had thickened by the time we reached the castle and we could no longer see the river below from the parapet. We were suspended in cloud.

The hostel was astir with noise and light. Wandering

into the common room, we saw that Phil and Mike were playing cards with two German girls who were in my dormitory.

'We're teaching the girls to play gin rummy,' said Mike.

The girls giggled.

'We are not very quick pupils,' said one.

We sat near them, half watching, speaking to them from time to time, talking to one another mostly. In the midst of all the people, James and I were together. Eventually someone started to strum a guitar, someone else to sing. No more was said that day about going to Strathcarron, by anyone. I went to bed feeling that I must be gaining in the battle for self-restraint since I had been dying to bring the subject up. I was itching to go there, now that we were so close, but it had become a delicate matter with James, because of Phil. A pity probably that we'd met up with him. Or was it? I seldom regret meeting anyone. And I liked Phil. Also, I would be quite happy to go up Strathcarron with him as part of the company, but James would not. I lay in my bunk with my thoughts going ding-dong through my head. Sleep came, releasing me, for I was exhausted right to the marrow of my bones. After all, it had been some journey to get here! As my granny says, you don't get anything for nothing in this world, and you're making a sad mistake if you expect it. Sometimes it happens of course, but that's a bonus.

The morning was dry, remarkably. It was not sunny, the sky was gey dreich looking, as Granny would have put it, but sun would have been a bit much to hope for after what we'd been through the day before. I stood in the courtyard with my face upturned and not a drop of moisture touched it.

'It's not cold either.'

James smiled. 'You want to go to Greenyards then?'

'I wouldn't be averse to the idea.'

'Okay, let's go. We'll take a picnic, shall we?'

When we went into the kitchen to make up our picnic, there were the Canadian boys cutting bread and spreading it with peanut butter.

Mike made a face. 'I am being being dragged to Glencalvie today to pay homage to Phil's forbears. Are you making the trip too?'

We could not deny it.

'We're just about ready for off,' said Phil. 'Coming, Mike? Maybe see you along the way somewhere,' he added casually to us.

I thought he was deliberately trying to get out of our way and was grateful. But I was also disappointed since I had expected that he would propose we all went together. Really, McKinley, you are muddled! I dressed myself down, then concentrated on the making of sandwiches.

Before we set off, I pinned my Cairngorm brooch to my shirt, the one that Margaret Ross had carried from Greenyards in 1854.

My calves ached excruciatingly after all that cycling to which I was not accustomed, and when I got back on the bike again I thought I'd never pedal more than a few yards without collapsing. James urged me on in true Fraser manner telling me there was nothing to it, it was all in the mind. I was quite prepared to believe it, but with a mind like mine what were you supposed to do? I really felt I'd done enough cycling and was going off the whole idea fast, if I could ever consider to have been on it. In fact, as I bounced over rutted bits of road, I realised that almost every part of my body was aching.

There was no sign of the Canadian boys on the road down to Ardgay where the turning goes off to Strath-carron. They must have got a lift. I gnashed my teeth at the thought of it since I had just hit a nasty stone and all but bitten the dust. Not that there was any dust to bite, only mud.

We reached the signpost, and I felt better at once when I saw the name of Greenyards. I raised a cheer, swerved, fell off.

'Honestly, Maggie!' James raised me up.

I must have been a terrible trial to him. His family were all so energetic and athletic, running up and down mountains, never putting a foot wrong, skiing effortlessly, swimming as though they'd been born in water. In sane moments he must have wondered how he'd ever got tangled up with me. Tangled was the word for me right then with the bicycle. I disengaged my left leg and James straightened out the front wheel. I feared that Catriona's machine would never be the same again. Still, she wouldn't have much need of a bicycle in the next few years.

We proceeded. Now that we were on the actual road to Greenyards I felt completely alert. Eyes, nose, ears were twitching, like a dog on a scent. I didn't want to miss anything. Margaret Ross, with a red shawl over her head and perhaps humming a tune to herself, must have walked this road many times as a girl. It probably hadn't changed all that much. There were trees on either side, a hill on our left. We passed two cottages on our right, one on the left, then the big gates of Gledfield House which had two animals perched on top that looked like howling wolves. They were nasty looking bits of work, might have been put there to keep evil spirits at bay. I caught a glimpse of a tree-lined drive with splashes of mauve rhododendrons. We cycled along beside the stone wall of the estate, soon leaving it behind. There were trees in abundance. James pointed out to me hawthorn, oak, birch, firs, copper beech. He always concluded, rightly, that as a city-slicker, I knew next to nothing about the

54

country. I think trees are great but can seldom tell their names. The fields looked quite lush and good, becoming scrubbier the further we went up the glen. Beyond, lay low heather-covered hills. It was a lonely, isolated scene. In Margaret's day there would have been more people around for the population had declined enormously since the middle of the nineteenth century. All that we saw were sheep, except when one tractor passed us. The man waved.

Now we had a heather moor on our left, with yellow gorse adding bright touches of colour. We were able to use a bit of colour, for the sky had been gradually taking on a deep leaden shade of grey and the wind had started to howl. I pulled up the hood of my anorak.

We rounded a corner, and there, seated in the lee of a dry-stone dyke, were Phil and Mike, munching peanut-butter sandwiches.

'Hi!' I cried, raising a hand in greeting. Well, needless to say, with my attention thus distracted, I swerved, hit a stone (there are always stones in the wrong places, deliberately placed, I feel), and fell off.

Chapter V

'Honestly, Maggie!' said James, as he pulled me up. Again!

'Machines and I were not designed for one another,' said I, trying to disengage myself from the bicycle wheel and retain my dignity (non-existent, I was beginning to think) at the same time. Difficult thing to do, especially since I had got one foot stuck through the chain. How I hate machinery! My jeans were all oil, mud, and dear knows what else, but that was of little importance. I wondered what my legs would look like underneath it all. If there was any part of me left unbruised by the end of this trip I'd be lucky. The beaches of Minorca were beginning to sound attractive. Lazy sun-filled days, smooth brown *unbruised* limbs .... Ah, those ads! Those glossy brochures!

Well, we were so far removed from that kind of scene that there was no point in thinking about it. Phil and Mike moved over to give me a nice flat seat beside them in the ditch.

'Have a sandwich,' said Mike. 'Peanut butter's a great healer.'

I accepted. Hunger had caught up with me. After his initial exasperation, James asked if I was all right. I was fine, fine, I declared, waving my peanut butter sandwich in the air, I'd never felt better, and I was thinking that perhaps I should hire myself out as a stuntwoman and get a job in films falling off motor bikes and the like since I seemed to have a talent for it. They wouldn't have to waste time training me: I was a natural. At least I made the Canadian boys laugh and James smile. James was busy untwisting the bicycle so laughing might have been difficult for him. His hands were clarty with oil from the knackered chain.

We ate our lunch, leaving a few sandwiches for later.

It was unavoidable that we should go on together. I decided that I would prefer to walk so James said okay, he would too, and proposed we leave the bicycles tucked away somewhere behind a wall. It was unlikely that many people would come this way, and those who did would not be potential bicycle thieves. Certainly no one would fancy nicking Catriona's now. I might have left a tip beside it if I'd thought there was any chance.

We got rid of the infernal things and took to the road on foot. Immediately I felt better. Liberated!

We tramped along singing 'Tipperary' and 'Keep Right On to the End of the Road'. For a while we had moorland on our left, the river remaining on our right all the time, and then we came into a lusher patch.

'I think we're approaching Greenyards,' said James.

We were approaching a large house, a private lodge. A big sign announced that clearly. Its name was Gruinards Lodge. There was a fat clump of lilac rhododendron beside the gate, birch flanking the drive, and looking up it I saw purple rhododendron on the left, and two small copper beeches sitting on a triangle where the drive forked. It was all very well cared for, and smooth, and seemed to have little to do with my vision of poor crofts and women fleeing wounded from the sheriff and his men. James said that the house might have been built after the Clearance, in the late nineteenth century. It was possible that some of the crofts had been on its ground. We went round the fence a little and came to a side gate through which we saw the house, which looked very large to me to be called a lodge (James said, 'It's for shooting, idiot, it's that kind of lodge!') and had treacle-brown wood trim round it that matched the fence. There was a post box in the wall that said 'Gruinards', and had one collection a day. I wished I'd brought a card to send to my granny from here.

The grass running down to the river was green and lush. It was easy to see where the name had come from and in the days before the eviction the land must have been fine to work and good for grazing the few beasts the families kept. Sheep moved slowly on the fields. It was for sheep that the Clearances had begun; no, that is not true, it was for the men who wanted to make money by keeping sheep. I told Mike how the Rosses had been evicted; James and Phil knew quite a bit themselves already.

'The sheriff and his men came over the hill from Tain, over there, during the night to evict the people. They came in carts and they'd been drinking so they were in an excitable kind of state. But the Ross women were ready for them, they had put their red shawls over their heads and they lined the road to block their way.'

'Not the men?'

'The men were either away, or feared. Apart from two or three, and they took to the hills as soon as the trouble started.'

'I guess women are the stronger sex,' said Mike. 'You won't catch me denying that!'

'The women stood their ground and were clubbed and beaten.' I was getting carried away: I could feel it all happening, see the women, their red shawls, the sheriff's men, hear the cries. 'Some had their heads broken, others their arms and legs. Young girls, and mothers of four and five children. Their blood ran and formed pools on the banks of the Carron. And the dogs came and licked it up.'

'Gee! Not a very nice story is it?'

Not at all.

We wandered further along. I imagined Margaret Ross and her wounded sister Agnes lying under cover, waiting for darkness to come so that they could begin their painful journey south. And I had been complaining about having to ride a bicycle! Maggie McKinley, you don't know you're born! I grinned, remembering my mother saying that to me many a time.

We came to a school sign. So there was still a school operating here, with children coming to shout and laugh along the road. Maybe not for long, said James: these small schools were dying out. Their cottage in Inverness-shire had once been a school. My own granny had gone there as a pupil. Once we'd passed the school we had more heather moor on our left, no use even for sheep; and always on our right ran the river. I had my eyes skinned for the remains of old cottages. We saw two or three that had been roofed over recently that might have been cleared in the nineteenth century, but none that *said* anything to me.

'What are you hoping to find?' asked James, with a smile. 'The remains of a cottage saying: "Margaret Ross lived here"?'

'Look!' I cried, pointing.

Ahead of us, on the river side, set back a little from the road, was the ruin of a cottage. All four walls were standing, the roof was gone, but not the chimney stacks, and even one chimney pot still stood. There were barns nearby, obviously in use.

I clambered over the fence and began to run. The ground was very marshy, making me slither and slide, and at times I had to jump the wettest looking bits.

Panting, excited, I reached it. It was a typical cottage

of the area, one-storeyed, with a central doorway and a window on either side, and it had been built of grey stone and harled. Some of the harling remained but it had gone mostly on the weather side. I stood and looked at it. I was sure that this was the cottage where my great-great-granny had lived: I felt it in my bones. As good a place as any to feel things in, says my granny.

The lintel over the doorway was still intact, though cracked. I went inside.

In the back wall were two windows also, looking out on to a green sward where sheep were grazing, and a line of trees that marked the course of the river. I couldn't see the water itself from here. The floor was covered over with weeds of course, but poking amongst them I found several things. The remains of an old iron bedstead, part of an old range, a bit of oven door, a green bottle and the skeletal remains of a sheep's head. Each find thrilled me. Margaret Ross might have slept in that bed! She might have cooked in that oven. At either end, you could see where fireplaces had been. I imagined them baking oatcakes on their griddle, an old black kettle singing on the hob. . . .

Looking up, I saw a bird was nesting in one chimney. So there was new life here again! That was good.

I leant out of one of the back windows. It was peaceful: no crying or lamenting, no barking of dogs, no blood on the green grass. And I felt comforted for Margaret Ross in a way, for more than a hundred years later one of her descendants had come back and found the place of her birth. And she herself had had a good rounded life in the end, living to be nearly eighty and having many children by the man she had met in Inverness-shire. It was poor Agnes who had died. But life goes on and is full of so many things. Different things. And often many that you don't expect. Standing there, I was pleased that I did not know what would happen to me in my life. I did not want to know.

'Can I come in?'

I turned to see James in the doorway. 'Be my guest! Isn't it marvellous, James, to have found it?'

'But you can't be sure, can you?'

'How do you mean?'

'That it's *your* Margaret Ross's cottage. I know it must have been a cottage belonging to a Ross but the chances are—'

'It doesn't matter whether it was actually hers or not. It might have been, and that's good enough for me. Don't you see?'

But he obviously didn't. I felt a real breakdown in communication with James then. I could not explain to him. Of course I knew it was not possible to trace the exact cottage, it might no longer exist, and there had been several Margaret Rosses, but, as far as I was concerned, I had found the home of my great-great-granny. I required no further evidence.

James came to stand beside me and look out at the hills.

'I was thinking, standing here,' I said.

'What about?'

'Oh, life and all that. You've got a pretty good idea what your life will be like, haven't you?'

'Have I?'

'It's planned, isn't it?'

'Well, up to a point. But there's always fate.' He grinned, clearly not believing that would play much part in his life. 'You are feeling philosophical, aren't you? Because of being here?'

'Perhaps.'

'Would you fancy living here? Working a croft?'

I knew that I couldn't, no longer had any illusions on that score. This place was too under-populated for me, and too far from my centre. And my centre? Glasgow of course. I don't even mean it was too far in terms of miles, just in the kind of life it had to offer. Even though I'd leave Glasgow and perhaps not live there again after I'd gone to university, I knew it would always be a bit of me. It had helped form me, I suppose. And it would provide my terms of reference. I felt so incredibly and unusually *perceptive* standing there in the shell of that old stone cottage, up to my ankles in wet weeds, that I was quite overwhelmed. It was almost as if someone else was talking to me. 'Those are moments of truth, Maggie,' Mr Scott had once said to me. Pity we don't get them more often. Usually I feel as if I'm fumbling my way through fog. But although this place might not be a part of my centre, it certainly meant something to me. It was a bit of my heritage. I was glad I'd come to seek it out: something in me was satisfied.

'I don't think I'm cut out for the homespun life,' I said. 'I *might* observe others at it, even visit, but—'

'It's raining,' said James.

So it was. We left the cottage for a nearby barn that had been re-roofed. It must be used by a local farmer. Phil and Mike were already there. The glen darkened alarmingly quickly; it was like someone dousing the lights. Clouds dropped down over the hills and rain washed the landscape with long sweeping lashes. We huddled inside the doorway, with anorak hoods up. I felt slightly hypnotised by the rain. There's something about heavy rain that sends shivers up and down my spine. Pleasant shivers. We did not talk.

When the rain slackened, we emerged. The sky now was lightening, and colour creeping back into the land. Before leaving the habitation, we had a look round the back of the cottage and discovered a black wheel that looked as if it might have come off an old sewing machine and, in a lean-to shed which had a burnt lintel over its doorway, some old pots, a bit of earthenware and an old broom-head.

'Brings the family close to you, doesn't it?' said Phil. 'Seeing these old things.'

I nodded. It brought him close to me to hear him saying that. I wanted to take something away with me. The pots were ready to disintegrate, the earthenware fragment was sharp, the sewing-machine wheel too heavy, so it had to be the brush-head.

'Are you going to take that with you?' said James.

'Looks kind of soggy to me,' said Mike.

'It's a relic of their domestic culture,' said I. 'And you can see it is not the same as a modern broom-head. They probably bought it from an itinerant pedlar. Shall we go on to Croick now?'

We squelched our way back to the road. I parked my memento behind the dyke to be collected on the way back.

The road twisted and turned, the glen becoming bleaker and the land looking scrubbier and incapable of supporting any crop. And then we saw a church. It stood on a lonely spot up away from the river, with no trees around it.

'That can't be it,' said Phil. 'The church at Croick has trees round it.'

We went up to the church and found the door open. Inside the porch stood a small table covered with a white cloth on which lay a few silver coins. So people came by sometimes, and presumably someone came too to take the money. Inside a wooden box we found communion plate, two pewter goblets, two empty bottles of invalid port and aluminium coins. We picked some up to look at them. Croick 1842, they said.

'Crofters would have been paid with these wouldn't

they, James?' I said. 'Tokens, instead of money. They'd trade with them, and bring them to the church as offerings.'

1842. It was as if life had stopped at that moment, like the hands of a clock shattered at the time of an accident. It was when the first shot had been fired, metaphorically speaking, that is, in the battle for the clearing of the glen. A notice had appeared on 9th February, 1842, in the *Inverness-shire Courier* about farms to be let on the estates of Glencalvie and Greenyards. Mr Fraser and I had read it all up. I wondered if Phil's great-great-grandfather and my great-great-granny had been able to read.

'Probably not,' said Phil. 'But the word must soon have gotten round.' That kind of word would have flown on wings from one end of the glen to the other.

We went into the auditorium. The walls were panelled with unvarnished pine and the windows of clear glass through which we could see the hills and river. A purple cloth covered the round pulpit and on it lay a bible and psalm book. Nowhere was there a name, or any word of any kind.

'It must have been the Free Church,' said James. 'The Free Presbyterian Church of Scotland,' he explained to the boys. 'They broke away from the Church of Scotland. They don't believe in ornament and they sing hymns without music.'

There was no piano or organ, no electricity either. Paraffin lamps on brackets were hung on the walls. It was bare and eerie because of the lack of human touch. The rain had come on again, closing us in. I shivered. Unpleasant shivers this time. I find deserted churches disturbing.

As soon as the rain stopped we moved on, crossing the river by a small bridge, continuing then on the opposite bank. A short way along, the Carron branched off; we were left with its tributary the Black Water. We passed a farm and came to the Presbyterian church at Croick which lay in a dip, well sheltered by the trees in its graveyard. We went down the grassy drive.

Phil ran in front of us. He didn't go into the church but round the side, looking for the diamond-paned east window on which the Glencalvie people had scratched their names and messages during their cold nights in the graveyard after their eviction.

'Look!' he cried.

We joined him, and peered at the scratchings on the window.

'"Glencalvie people was in the church here May 24 1845,"' he read. '"John Ross shepherd. Amy Ross. Glencalvie people the wicked generation. Glencalvie is a wilderness. Blow ship them to the colony. . . ."'

The wind was rustling in the yews, sheep were bleating. Those sheep always seemed to be bleating and I couldn't have said that the sounds they made were joyful.

'About eighty-eight people were evicted from the glen,' said Phil, who had obviously, like me, been reading up on his ancestors. 'Twenty-three of them were children under ten and seven were ill. And one of them was my great-great-grandfather. His mother thought he wouldn't survive the cold and damp for even though it was May the weather was pretty bad.' He looked round the graveyard at the old stones and shook his head. 'Strange, coming here, seeing it. My granny used to tell me the story of their eviction and, you know, well it just seemed like a story. But now I can believe it.'

I understood. It was strange for me to think that his granny and my granny had been telling us similar stories all those hundreds of miles apart.

'Why the wicked generation?' asked Mike.

'They thought they must have been wicked to be

punished by God in this way,' said Phil. 'I suppose their religion taught them that.'

'What a scene!' said Mike. 'Put out of your house, have to sleep in the graveyard, and on top of it believe that it was only what you deserved! I'm glad I didn't live in the nineteenth century.'

'You could be put out of your home in places now,' said James.

'You're right,' said Phil.

'Maggie was,' said James.

Phil and Mike looked at me.

'Oh we didn't have to sleep in a graveyard. We were given a bright new modern flat in a high-rise block that nearly sent my mother round the twist. She's all right now,' I added. 'We had to leave though.'

It was cold and damp out there in the churchyard, and the sky was taking on that end-of-the-world aspect again. We went inside.

This church had brown varnished pews and cream-coloured walls and a piano! So they did have some music. We saw on a notice that the minister came once a year from Kincardine to take a service. It was darker than the interior of the other church, due to the surrounding trees, and the fact that it lay in a hollow, but I found it easier to be in because there was more sign that actual flesh and blood people still came around. There was a visitors' book for a start, and a pile of green sheets of paper telling you a bit about the church and the Glencalvie people. On the wall there was a greyish-white shield edged in red with a red deer in the centre. But, in spite of those few touches, it was still eerie and rather morose. You could feel the tragedy of those poor people hanging about the place. You could imagine their suffering and their feeling of helplessness as they huddled round the gravestones, not knowing where they would go, or what would happen to them. They had lost everything, they had no power, no influence anywhere. They were complete victims. You could think of nothing but their misery whilst you were in there.

The rain came again, darkening the church even more. I stood by the window looking out. It was a bleak spot and I would be happy to leave it. Phil wandered around examining every detail. I preferred Greenyards to this, it was brighter and lighter.

When it was dry again, Mike led the way out. He'd probably had enough of old Scottish doom-laden history. So possibly had James, but he was too polite to say so.

'Where to now?' asked Mike. 'Don't suppose there's a funfair anywhere in the vicinity? A ride on the Ghost Train would make a little light relief.'

'I'd sure like to take a *look* at Glencalvie,' said Phil. 'It's not far. And now that we've come—'

'Okay, okay,' said Mike, groaning. 'I reckoned this morning there'd be no escaping it.'

Before we went we sat on the wall and ate the rest of our picnic, or most of it, keeping some chocolate and biscuits and a packet of dates.

The road to Glencalvie was very pretty: narrow, with grass growing up the middle in places, and tree-lined. There were masses of firs and rhododendrons. Gorgeous! On either side we had forest: the Amat forest. We identified it on our map. I loved travelling by map, reading out the names of the hills, or trying to, for usually I couldn't say them since they were in Gaelic. *Meall Dheirgidh*!

Phil and Mike walked in front, James and I behind.

'I'm really enjoying myself,' I said.

'I'm glad,' he said, not sounding glad at all, not meaning to.

'What's up with you? You've a face on you like a soor

67

ploom.' I knew it annoyed him when I affected broad Scots.

'Thanks very much!'

'Don't mention it.'

A silly childish spat. Later, when we'd returned to civilisation, I did concede that he had been asked to bear too much of these pilgrimages. To go on mine had been enough for him, to be asked to go on Phil's also had been a bit thick. But right then we were having a clash of interests so I was unwilling to concede anything.

I wondered what time of day it would be but did not want to ask James in case it should turn out to be rather late and he might use that as an excuse to turn back. With clouds covering the sky, there was no way of knowing by the height of the sun. Not that I'm much use at that kind of scene. I never have a watch so go round oblivious of time, but have a good excuse when I'm late. Once I did own one, but usually forgot to wind it, and in the end lost it, infuriating my father who said I got everything too easily.

About a mile along the road we saw the ruins of a cottage down by the river. We stopped.

'That might have been *your* great-great-grandpa's,' said Mike to Phil.

'Guess it might. Though I believe most of them lived in turf cabins.'

'Easier to burn down,' I said.

Phil nodded. We stood and gazed down at the ruined cottage for a few minutes. I thought of the poor families scraping a living growing a bit of barley and oats, keeping a cow or two and a few sheep. It might not have been a rich life, but it was one they had wanted to hold on to.

'Shall we push on?' said Phil.

Mike groaned. 'We're not expected to go all the way up the glen, are we? We're miles from civilisation as it is.'

'No.' Phil smiled. 'I'd like to go just a little further

though.' He looked at James and me. 'If you're all willing?'

'I am,' said I.

'I don't mind,' said James.

We continued. The ground now was heather- and bracken-covered, with large mature pine trees. It was a great feeling going steadily further into the hills, not that we could see much of them since the tops were covered with low cloud. James said if we went far enough we'd come out at the west coast.

'I wouldn't mind doing that sometime,' I said.

'Not today,' said Mike.

The gates to Glencalvie Lodge came up on our left. After this point the road got much rockier, with pot-holes full of water, and the country got scrubbier. There were many fewer crofts here than further down Strathcarron in my great-great-granny's part. I thought Margaret Ross had known what she was doing living nearer the main road. I wondered if they'd ever gone anywhere from here, apart from the church at Croick on Sundays. The trees too were beginning to look a bit like the 'petrified forest' with trunks bleached white like bones and fallen branches lying on the ground all mangled and distorted. Rather weird. But the river was cheerful, rushing and gurgling – we were back with the Carron again – and the trees alongside it were still full of life.

Then James suggested we strike up through the forest on our right to the ridge, so that we could look down and get a better view of the glen.

'Good idea,' said Phil.

James and Phil went ahead now, Mike and I lagged a little in the rear. I noticed that we were gradually seeing even less of the hills: mist was descending, though nobody had even mentioned it. The going was more difficult through the woods, with bracken to slow us, fallen trees to climb over, and occasional fences to navigate. My legs were aching again.

'It's a long way back,' murmured Mike. 'And not much chance of a lift would you say?'

'Hardly. Unless there's a cart left over by the sheriff's men. A ghost cart.'

'Driven by the Dowager Duchess!'

We had a good laugh at that. Phil stopped to find out what was amusing us, James strode on. I took the chance to get my breath back. Suddenly, I felt really tired. I said so, collapsing on to a fallen tree trunk.

'Can't say I feel all that fresh myself,' said Mike, joining me.

'Okay,' said Phil. 'Perhaps we should call it a day. We've done a heck of a lot after all.'

'I reckon your ancestors can all sleep easy now,' said Mike.

We turned to look for James. There was no sign of him.

'James!' I called. I got up.

We listened. All that we heard was the bleat of some distant sheep. The mist was creeping in amongst the trees now, swirling and eddying.

'James!' I called again, more urgently.

Still no answer. James seemed to have disappeared.

Chapter 6

All together, we shouted James's name. We heard it dying away in amongst the trees. Our voices sounded like ghost voices.

'Come on,' said Phil. 'We'd better go after him. He may be waiting for us a bit further up.'

Was he annoyed by our little tiff? Is that why he had gone striding on?

We stumbled through the forest, climbing steadily upwards, keeping close together. The mist was thickening rapidly. I had a sick feeling in the pit of my stomach. Surely James would turn back soon and reappear out of the trees in front of us? He wasn't such a fool as to go pressing on out of annoyance, was he? He knew all about Scottish hills and the freaky weather conditions that could arise so quickly. People were lost every summer, as well as in the winter months. It had been damp all day, so the mist was no particular surprise.

We had another halt and Mike produced a bar of chocolate. We bunched together as we ate, each thinking our own thoughts, but saying nothing. I noticed Phil glancing at his watch.

'What time is it?' I asked.

'Eight.'

'*Eight*?'

'Well, we've been messing around quite a bit and we didn't leave the hostel till ten this morning.'

I was silent. That horrid, clammy, moving mist seemed to be gaining every minute. Normally it wasn't dark up here till about eleven at this time of year, but with such an overcast day one couldn't rely on that. It might well be dark even about nine or a little after.

'Let's shout again,' I said.

We shouted, over and over again. We heard only sheep in return, though where they were I couldn't imagine. Not inside the forest surely.

'I wish they'd shut up,' I said. 'The sheep.' They were getting on my nerves, always giving off the same mournful note. Coming out of the mist it sounded even worse. And the trees were now beginning to look like ghosts. I had ghosts on the brain!

'There's no point in going on,' said Phil. 'We could go for miles and the mist's getting thicker. We'll have to turn back.'

'We can't abandon him,' I wailed.

'We're not abandoning him, Maggie,' said Phil gently. 'But there's nothing we can do. And he's used to hills and mountains, isn't he?'

It was true: James was an experienced hill and mountain walker, he would know what to do, how to tackle a situation such as this, whereas the three of us were complete dumbheads. We gave one last shout. We listened to the echo of our own voices.

'Hey,' said Mike, 'just a minute! I've a feeling we're near the top of the ridge. Let's press on a little.'

We pressed on, with Mike leading the way, me in the middle, and Phil bringing up the rear.

'We *are* at the top!' said Mike. 'The ground's starting to go down again.'

We were clear of forest too now, back with heather and boulders. And sheep. They were bleating on every side. Maybe they didn't like the mist any more than we did.

We descended. I did not ask whether it was a good idea, or where it would be taking us, I merely followed Mike. Phil whistled cheerfully behind me and I was glad of the sound, otherwise the sheep would have had total monopoly, and by the time I emerged from this wilderness I'd have had the screaming heebie-jeebies. If we ever did emerge. Visibility was lessening all the time.

I stumbled over a stone, Phil caught my elbows from behind and steadied me. I felt all but done in.

'Mike,' called Phil. 'Wait!'

Mike came back to us.

'Think we should take a breather for a minute. Maggie's finding the pace a bit much.'

'Sorry,' said Mike. 'I keep forgetting our legs are longer.'

'It's okay.' Even if my legs had been ten feet long I'd have been knackered.

After a couple of minutes the boys decided we'd better get moving again. Time was getting on – it now showed nine on Phil's illuminated watch dial – and we didn't want to have to spend the night in the open.

I forced my aching legs onwards. Phil went first this time. We kept much closer to one another for shortly it was not going to be possible to see more than an arm's length ahead. I kept thinking about James. Imagine being alone in this! I shuddered.

It was growing rapidly darker. And colder. Phil became a blurred shape in front of me. We bungled along, stopping every few yards to exchange a few words. The ground was so rough that each of us stumbled to our knees from time to time. I knew my feet and legs must be soaking wet but was so numbed that I couldn't feel it.

Now there was little light left at all, and there would be no chance of a moon unless a stiff wind blew up and dispersed the mist. I couldn't feel the faintest stirring of a breeze. That driving wind that had swept through Strathcarron earlier had well and truly blown itself out.

'"Keep right on to the end of the road,"' I sang, or tried to, but my voice petered out quickly. There was no road to keep on, only an invisible, obstacle-stacked hillside.

Phil stopped suddenly; I stumbled over him, and Mike stumbled over me. The three stooges. Only we didn't feel very comical.

'I guess we're really and truly lost,' said Phil.

'You don't say!' said Mike. 'Phil Ross, you amaze me!'

'The thing we mustn't do,' said Phil, 'is panic.'

I didn't feel much like panicking. I was too exhausted, only wanted to sink down on the ground and pass out. We mustn't do that either, Phil said, or we might expire from exposure. It was August, I protested, not January.

'You couldn't say the heat was overpowering though, could you?' said Mike.

No, I could not, especially since my teeth were chattering quite audibly. We clustered close to one another to increase our body warmth and Mike fished out some gluey dates which he declared would renew our energy. I'd have needed a crateful to do that but they did at least stop my teeth chattering.

We must find some shelter, even if it was a half-ruined cottage. If we could just find somewhere to hole up, it would start to get light again in a few hours. The warden at the hostel would be worrying about us but we had to put that out of our minds since there was nothing we could do about it.

'They wouldn't send a search party out at night,' said Phil.

James was not so easy to put out of our minds.

'He might be hurt,' I said.

'And he might be back in civilisation raising the alarm,' said Phil. 'He might have got back down on to the road from the forest.'

Yes, he might. I decided I'd better think that way.

'Better to think positively,' said Mike. 'Ha, ha! Can't say I feel all that positive at this moment.'

'We have to think our way out of these hills,' said Phil.

'Glencalvie!' said Mike. 'Don't ever say that name to me once we get out of here. Can't you call up some old ancestral ghost, Phil, to show us the way through the mist? Are you there, Great-great-grandpapa?'

'Oh shut up! Come on,' said Phil, with new determination. 'Let's move.'

'Onward the Rosses!' cried I. Margaret wouldn't have faltered. Clotted with blood, she had carried sister Agnes on her back through the hills. How soft I was in comparison! If I didn't get my food regularly I was ready to faint.

We joined hands and floundered on through the darkness and mist. Downwards. It was an odd sensation moving downward in the dark. Every minute I expected to plunge into an abyss. Phil said that wasn't possible: this was a low hill. To me, it felt like Ben Nevis.

I think now, looking back, that after a while we must have become not only physically exhausted but mentally dazed. We careered mindlessly on. We seemed to have it in our minds that we must not stop, that as long as we were moving we would get somewhere. Afterwards, we were told it would have been better to have huddled together against a rock or dyke and waited, for it was unlikely that we would have suffered much from exposure when there were three of us to generate heat. But, in fact, we encountered no dykes or large enough rocks.

On, on, on, dragging one foot after the other. I can't remember if I thought of anything. Possibly not. Occasionally pictures flashed before my mind. James's face. My mother's. My granny's. I had one moment of real panic. I thought maybe I was going to die. I cried out.

'It's all right, Maggie,' said Phil, somewhere in the darkness. His hand tightened round mine.

'I can't go on, I can't.' My knees gave way.

'We'll have to stop, Phil.'

'Yes, okay.'

We were all on the ground. What a relief! I didn't care about getting anywhere, just as long as I didn't have to stand upright again.

'I can hear water,' said Phil. 'Listen! It's a river.'

'Up!' said Mike.

They hauled me up. I didn't see why the river was so important.

When we reached the river we were actually able to see it: we saw the water glinting. And we could certainly hear it; the noise was enormous.

'Must be a waterfall,' murmured Mike.

'How're we to get across?' said Phil.

Not by jumping anyway, and wading seemed kind of out, unless you were a masochist. It seemed pretty wide, said Mike. What did we have to cross it for at all, I wanted to know, but they appeared to think that rivers were there to be crossed. We stood for ages staring at the dark running water, listening to its roar. I was beginning to feel hypnotised by the sound.

Mike and Phil decided we should follow it along; it was bound to come out somewhere. Sound judgment that!

'Don't go too close,' said Phil. 'You wouldn't want to fall in.'

I needed no convincing on that point. I gave it a wide berth and staggered around, making no progress in ground that appeared to be totally whin-covered.

'Give me your hand, Maggie,' said Phil.

Mike was ahead, but only by a yard. We had agreed that on no account must any of us leave the sight of the others even for a second. A second was enough in which to get lost. Look at James!

'I think I've found a bridge,' cried out Mike excitedly.

A bridge! Civilisation? Phil and I reached him. He was fumbling around with his arms, spreading them out the way kids do when playing Blind Man's Bluff.

'Do be careful,' said Phil. 'You're awfully near the edge.'

'It *is* a bridge. Wooden.'

'Could it be a sheep bridge?' said Phil.

I supposed that it could, but knew too little about country matters to be sure. Later, we were told that that was what it was.

'Should we go over?' said Mike.

'Guess so,' said Phil. 'Might lead to a farm.'

We joined hands. The bridge might be rotten, I thought, or even end in the middle like that one at Avignon. How could we be sure it would straddle the river? We couldn't. We had to have some faith, trust to luck. I said nothing. No doubt the boys had their own doubts about crossing an unknown bridge in darkness also.

Slowly, we edged across. The river sounded furious, boiling below us. How deafening is the sound of water!

Mike stopped. 'Something here. Just a minute. . . . It's a gate.'

'Can you get it open?' asked Phil.

'It's tied. Can't seem to. . . .' Mike wrestled for a moment, then said he would climb over. He did. 'Dry land!' he declared.

It was not really dry, being rather marshy, but it was land and not the middle of the river. We stood on the bank feeling that we had achieved something. Though what? The scene didn't seem to be any different on this side, no sign of farms or lights or any other aspect of civilisation.

'What now?' I asked.

On, of course. We fumbled our way through heather and marsh, tripped over rocks. Mostly, we went close to the river; sometimes we found what appeared to be a bit of track that took us a little away from it. I lost all sense of what was happening or what we were supposed to be doing.

'We're going up a bit again,' said Phil.

Up or down, I didn't care, didn't question. From time to time I sat down and they pulled me to my feet again.

'There's a wall here!' shouted Phil, who was in the lead. 'I can feel it.'

A wall? Was that a matter for celebration? I sat down again, let my head fall back, and I felt the wall. It was kind of hard, stony, jaggy.

'Come on, Maggie,' said Mike.

His voice sounded a long way away. I rested on the edge of oblivion. Everything was sliding and tilting.

'Maggie, wake up!' They were shaking me. 'Come on, we're going to follow the wall round.'

I groaned, protested, tried to slide back into sleep. I didn't care if they'd found the Great Wall of China. They shook me again and again, remorselessly. They were brutes. I told them so. I told them to leave me. Let me sleep in peace. They could go where they wanted. They paid no attention to me.

'I can't stand up.' I tried. My knees crumbled.

'Get on to your hands and knees.'

I obeyed.

'Now move! Move, Maggie, and keep moving.'

So we crawled our way round the perimeter of the wall. At the time I couldn't see the point in it, nor did I try to. I just did it, and whenever I stopped I was prodded in the rear. Otherwise, I'd have gone to sleep ten times over.

'There's a break in the wall. A gate! Iron.'

'It may be a lodge.'

At that I perked up. The fog inside my head cleared a little. A lodge meant light and warmth, food, and maybe even a soft bed. A bed! They yanked me to my feet. I remember thinking that perhaps I had been struck down by blindness. I couldn't seem to see anything.

'Can you get the gate open?'

The gate swung open. Tentatively, we moved forward.

'We're on grass.'

Maybe it was just a field. My hopes drooped.

'There's something here,' said Phil slowly. 'I can feel something.'

Thank goodness for that. As long as it wasn't a sheep!

'What is it?' said Mike.

'I think. . . . Yes, it is! It's a tombstone!'

Chapter 7

We had arrived back at the Presbyterian church at Croick, the one where Phil's ancestors had spent the night after their eviction.

'History repeats itself!' said Mike. 'So whadya know?'

We didn't actually spend the night amongst the gravestones, nor did we scratch messages on the windows, but we did pass the night, or what was left of it, in the church. We tried at first to lie on the pews but they were much too narrow, even for me, and were made of wood that felt harder than the ground. No cushions on them or anything pansyish like that. So we abandoned them for the floor which at least had matting to soften it a little.

I passed out immediately.

My sleep was not peaceful, being full of dreams in which I was wandering around in mist and rain crying out James's name. From time to time I woke, but quickly sank back down again. Finally, I sat up, cold and stiff, as dawn was creeping into the church. It was a grey, watery dawn, completely quiet, which was weird. There were no birds singing, no sheep bleating. Mike and Phil still slept, sprawled awkwardly on the hard floor. Clothes tousled, hair tangled, faces smeared with dirt, they looked like tramps.

I lay back and let my eyes rest on the ceiling. This was a very strange place in which to have spent a night.

But James? Where was he? The thought came,

piercing me like a sharp knife. He might be wandering, dazed, still lost, or he might be lying hurt, bleeding, needing help; or he might, though I scarcely dared think this, be dead. Of course he couldn't be dead! He was too sensible to die on a Scottish hill. Things like that didn't happen to him. Things like that didn't happen to Frasers. Now if it were me, Maggie McKinley, bumbling her way round. . . .

Urgently, I roused the boys. We must get help for James.

We blinked as we emerged into the cold morning light. Dew lay thick on the churchyard grass, and in the yew trees a bird was trying a few chirps. It sounded unsure of itself, in its first notes, just as we felt. We staggered up the drive on to the road. My legs felt as if they were stuffed with straw, aching straw. But the mist had gone, mercifully. I never wanted to see mist again.

It was no distance to the nearest farm. We were able to phone for help from there, and not long afterwards a police car arrived. Whilst we waited the farmer's wife gave us tea and hot toast. Our throats were so parched we could scarcely swallow.

When the police came they wanted us to give them an exact description of where we had been, last sighted James, etc. He had not found his way back to civilisation himself. Somehow, I had not expected it. We did our best, each of us finding the others' versions not quite right. It was like the witnesses of an accident all having different stories. But it *had* been misty, of course, and we'd done a lot of floundering.

'Somewhere up Glencalvie,' said Phil.

'Glencalvie,' groaned Mike. 'Never suggest taking me there again!'

'The Amat Forest,' I said.

The police were organising a search party. I asked if we

couldn't come but they didn't seem to think we would be much use and besides, we were on our last legs, as one of them said. Just look at us! We had to admit, looking at one another, that we were pretty rough looking. It was to be back to the hostel and bed for us.

They drove us to Carbisdale where the warden was relieved to see us. He hadn't slept much the night before either.

I staggered up to my dormitory, which was empty at this time of day. A bath might have been in order but I would have passed out in it, I felt sure. I pulled off my boots and filthy jeans and crawled into my sleeping bag. Sleep would not come. I couldn't get James out of my mind. If anything had happened to him – anything serious – I would feel terrible. And I would feel guilty. Yes, I would feel guilty. If I'd been nicer to him and less determined to get my own way, he wouldn't have gone off like that. It was all my fault.

If he was to die. . . . Don't be silly, I told myself. But people did die, and James might have been hurt. He *might* be dead now. I buried my face in my pillow. Poor, poor James.

Dinne be so daft, lassie! I could almost hear my granny speaking. *You musne think the worst till it happens.* I lifted my head thinking she must be in the room.

It was Phil whom I saw. He was standing in the doorway.

'Any news?' I cried out.

He shook his head, came a little way into the room. 'I just wanted to make sure you were okay.' He came closer. 'You're real fond of James, aren't you?'

'I suppose I must be. If anything—' And then, horror of horrors, I began to cry, right in front of Phil! I do know how to choose my times.

Phil comforted me. He was dead nice; he put his arm

round my shoulders and talked to me gently and sensibly, saying he felt sure they'd find James pretty soon and James was a pretty tough guy so I shouldn't really think anything bad had happened to him.

I dried my tears and blew my nose.

'Now you try to get some sleep and I'll let you know the minute there's any news. Right?'

I nodded. He went out and I went to sleep.

When I wakened, Phil was there again, standing beside my bunk.

'They've found James.'

'Oh thank goodness! Is he all right?'

'Concussed.'

I jerked bolt upright, almost overturning the bunk. Phil steadied it.

'He's unconscious then? He must have been hurt?'

'Seems he hit his head.'

Head injury. Brain damage. My mind does make some fantastic leaps at times. Phil calmed me, telling me that people often have concussion and are none the worse for it afterwards. The hospital had been cagey and wouldn't tell Phil much over the telephone. That was understandable since Phil was only a holiday acquaintance of James's. They wanted the names and addresses of James's next of kin. I would have to supply that.

Hurriedly, I washed and dressed, and before we left for the hospital, which was at Golspie, further up the coast, the boys insisted that I had a decent meal. Mike had cooked it.

Also, they came with me. It was a fair way to Golspie, about twenty miles, but that was the nearest hospital apparently, apart from old folks' homes which were hardly what had been needed in this case. There was a bus service of sorts but the boys said we'd be quicker hitching.

We got a lift from the hostel to the road end at Ardgay, then walked from there across the bridge over the mouth of the River Shin to the township of Bonar Bridge. Now we were in Sutherland. That didn't mean much to me right then: I only wanted to get to Golspie.

It was late afternoon. Quite a lot of traffic was still going through but most of it was comprised of tourists' cars laden to the gills, and the odd couple who passed probably didn't fancy the three of us for company on their holiday. I couldn't blame them, but I was beginning to feel desperate.

'There's a north-bound train leaving Ardgay about six-thirty,' said Phil. 'If all else fails we'll have to go back and get that.'

All else did not fail for, at that moment, a car drew up with one nice man in it. And he was going to Brora, on past Golspie. By the time we reached the hospital I thought I was going to be sick.

'Take a deep breath, Maggie,' said Phil.

'You look like the Duchess's ghost,' said Mike.

That made me smile. The sickness ebbed. We went inside.

James had recovered consciousness! The sister took me to the ward. And there, lying propped against pillows, a bandage round his head, was James. When he saw me, he smiled.

'James!' I rushed forward and kissed him.

'Gently,' said the sister, before she disappeared.

I bombarded him with questions. What had happened to him? Had he hit his head? When did he realise he was lost? He remembered little, only slipping, falling, striking his head. After that, he had been unconscious, surfacing for brief bewildering moments. It was like a dream to him now, a bad one, of course.

'That should put you off hill-walking for a bit!'

It would do nothing of the kind, and I might have known it, for it would take more than being knocked unconscious and spending a night on a hillside to put him off. I groaned. So I wasn't going to get out of all that hectic outdoor stuff so easily! There would be future occasions in my life when I'd be slogging over moors and up hillsides with my legs caught in heather and my breath cutting me like a pain between my ribs.

'That's right,' said James.

You had to hand it to the Frasers: they were tough and they didn't give up. No sir!

I sat on the edge of James's bed and held his hand. I told him that his mother was going to have to be notified.

He groaned. 'You know what'll happen, don't you?'

Only too well. James said I must try to get in touch with his parents myself and tell them that he was all right, and they were not to come. I promised, but wasn't exactly hopeful that they'd believe me. At least his mother wouldn't. What a summer she was having! A far cry from the two months' rural peace she had been anticipating.

The sister came to eject me after half an hour. James protested that he wasn't at all tired but I could see that the colour had gone from his face during the time I'd been with him. Normally he looks ruddy and healthy, now he was grey around the eyes and his skin almost sallow. Almost like me, in fact. I told him that and made him laugh. He put his hands over his ribs.

'Do they hurt?' asked the sister.

'No,' he said. 'Not at all.'

'See you tomorrow,' I said, blowing him a kiss.

Phil and Mike were waiting patiently, and wanted to know how James was. I told them he looked remarkably fit, considering.

'Good Scottish constitution, that's what it is,' said Mike, thumping himself on the chest and coughing.

'Wish I had one.'

'I thought all Canadians were tough and outdoorish too?'

'All Canadians are nothing,' said Phil.

I accepted the rebuke meekly.

Before leaving the hospital, I promised to contact James's parents. Since they were not on the telephone at the cottage, I would have to phone their local policeman, leaving a message for them to ring me at the hostel.

I rang Inverness-shire from Golspie, with the boys squashed into the box with me. To get out of the rain!

The constable was at home. I had a bit of a job over the crackly line to get the message to him *exact*. He's a trifle deaf and he kept repeating, 'He's lying up the glen the now?' Not the now, I explained, he *was*, but at this moment was in hospital being cared for, and there was nothing greatly to worry about. I wanted to convey the idea that the matter was urgent enough for the Frasers to phone, but not so urgent that they would panic.

'Dinne you worry, lass. I'll see to it.'

I replaced the receiver, feeling a shade off confident. I imagined him getting his old rusty bike out of the shed and pedalling off down the glen. And then I imagined Mrs Fraser getting her car out and driving north.

'I guess we'll have missed the last train south?' said Mike.

We went to the station to find out. Naturally, we had.

So it was back on the road for us again, where there was a noticeable lack of traffic queuing for our custom. The first lift we got took us half a mile along the road before it turned off into a farm, the second for about three miles before it, too, disappeared up a muddy track.

'At this rate,' said Mike, glancing at his watch, 'we shall be late back at the hostel. And the warden ain't going to like it!'

'Would you blame him?' said Phil.

As we walked we talked, the boys telling me a bit more about themselves and of Canada, and I told them about Glasgow and our family, and our plumbing business. I made them laugh with tales of Aunt Jessie and my mother.

'Sounds like you have good fun in your family,' said Phil.

'We're just a bundle of laughs a minute,' I said. Sometimes a bundle of disasters too, I refrained from adding.

A van was approaching. We stepped back to the side of the road; Mike lifted his thumb, and the van stopped. The driver said he was going to Inverness.

'Great!' cried Mike. 'Could you take us to Ardgay?'

He could, and did. We had to walk most of the way from there to the hostel – and by that time I felt as if my feet were made of raw meat – but we did get there by ten o'clock, one full hour before closing.

'There've been two phone calls for you, Maggie,' said the warden. 'From a Mrs Fraser. She said she'd try again later.'

About half an hour later he came looking for me in the common room. There was a phone call for me from Inverness-shire.

Chapter 8

Mrs Fraser rattled out a string of questions: how, when, where, why, what? I started to gabble about Greenyards and Croick until she interrupted me, which didn't take long.

'But how did James come to be lost in the mist?'

Well, it was a long story. 'You see, we were with these Canadian boys—'

She cut me off one more time, saying that I could tell her the rest when she came. For she was coming of course. First thing in the morning. I told her there was really no need, I could look after James, he didn't want her to have to bother, but she *had* to come, to see for herself.

That night I was filled with gloomy apprehension and didn't sleep as well as I'd expected after such a hectic day. My tossing and turning didn't do much for the girl under me. I kept thinking about Mrs Fraser and that if I didn't get up quickly enough she'd have James whipped away in the back of her car to Inverness-shire, or Edinburgh. She's that kind of woman: you have to be up early in the morning to outsmart her.

My intention was to get the first train north which departed from Ardgay at 7.58 a.m. The next one was at midday, so I couldn't afford to wait for that. I had told Phil and Mike I'd go alone.

I managed to get up at seven. I crawled down the hill and was in time for the train. It was due in Golspie at ten to nine. That should beat even Mrs Fraser.

Arriving at the hospital, the first thing I saw outside was the Frasers' car.

They were sitting, one on either side of James's bed. Mr smiled at me as I came in, but Mrs was too busy frowning to put forth any welcome signals.

'Hello, Maggie,' said James.

'James is being very stupid,' said his mother. 'He says he'll be able to go on with his holiday, I say he'll have to come home.'

'Now, Mother, stop fussing!'

'I'm not fussing.'

'Yes, you are.'

'You've been quite badly injured. . . .'

I gazed discreetly out of the window.

After a bit James began to wilt so she laid off and folded her lips into a tight line that made the skin round them pucker. There was a look on her face that suggested that she always had thought no good would come out of this holiday, and now she was proved right. Mr asked me how I was and said it must have been an ordeal for me to have been out all night on my own.

'She wasn't on her own,' said Mrs. 'Not as far as I've heard. You had two other boys with you, didn't you, Maggie?'

I blushed. I didn't know why I did and was furious with myself. It didn't mean anything either: it was just that Mrs Fraser had got me on the wrong foot and I'd felt all irritable and roughed up the wrong way.

James looked exhausted. His head lolled back on the pillow and I was beginning to wonder whether his mother might be right (perish the thought!) and that he should be taken home. We stayed another few minutes, then left him to sleep. On the way out the Frasers had a word with the doctor who said he was pleased with James's progress and saw no reason why he shouldn't be able to leave hospital in two or three days. As long as he didn't have a relapse. Brought on by his mother and me arguing over his bed for example?

'We shall stay in town,' said Mrs Fraser, 'and see how he gets on.'

What about me? asked Mr Fraser. I supposed I'd stay on at Carbisdale. My immediate plan was to take the middle of the day train back. Three trains a day doesn't give you much scope. I longed for James to be out of hospital and for us to be back on the road again together. Dear knows when we would get another chance to have a holiday on our own! At the end of the fortnight I had to go back to Glasgow and school, and there I would remain until Christmas.

I went with the Frasers to the hotel they had booked into, and had coffee with them. For a kick-off, Mrs gave me the third degree, then Mr stepped in and started asking me about Greenyards and Glencalvie. He was very interested, had been up to Strathcarron himself a few years back. He teaches history, you see, and knows a lot about the Clearances. Mrs sat and stared into space. Her eyes had that kind of remote look, slightly wistful, slightly apprehensive. I couldn't help feeling sorry for her after all.

Before I went for my train, I paid James another brief visit. This time, we were alone. Apart from the other three men in the ward, that is, but them I felt I could ignore, whereas Mrs Fraser was another matter.

I moved my chair as close as I could to the bed. We held hands. We sat and smiled into one another's eyes, and it reminded me of the way it used to be in Granny's glen last summer. James looked better too, after his morning's rest.

'What about Phil and Mike?' he asked. 'Have they gone on?'

'Not exactly.' Silly answer!

'How do you mean, not exactly?'

'Well, as a matter of fact, they're still there.'

James was silent, and the light in his eye seemed a little dimmed. I even felt a slackening in his fingers as they lay curled around mine.

'James, there's nothing to worry about with Phil and Mike. They're just two good friends.'

'You've only known them two or three days. How can they really be good friends?'

'Well, they are. They just are.'

And they were. It was strange to think that I had only known them for a few days, four in fact. I felt they had been part of my life for quite a long time. Perhaps you can't spend such a night as we had without forming some kind of bond. I said so to James.

'Ah yes, I'd forgotten you spent the night in the church with them.'

'James, for heaven's sake! You're not going to be jealous of *two* boys, are you?'

'I am not jealous.' He released my hand.

This was ridiculous. I felt irritation rising in me and I began to scratch. I'm always like this when I'm irritated, it's like having a rash, it affects my skin. James, who knew this, watched me scratching, his eyes cold. His eyes can be cold at times; at others, they can be soft and gentle.

One of these days I really would cultivate serenity and be disturbed by nothing. In a kind of heated cool, I told James he had absolutely nothing to worry about where the Canadian boys were concerned, and he was crazy to be jealous. Then I softened. After all, there he was lying in bed with nothing to do, thinking about me, wondering what I was up to, with his holiday spoiled, more or less. We had planned this trip to Easter Ross for such a long time and had seen it as some kind of idyllic dream.

'James, it's you I care about. Honest!'

He took my hand back and squeezed it hard.

I had to leave then; they were bringing round the injections and medicines and things. Anyway, I couldn't afford to miss my train, or else I'd have to wait hours for the next one.

I kissed him goodbye, and looked back from the door to smile at him. He smiled at me too. Everything was all right between us; we could survive a little storm occasionally.

The Frasers took me to the station.

'See you tomorrow, I expect, Maggie?' said Mr.

Yes, I expected that they would.

I enjoyed the train ride. It was great sitting there having nothing to do but look out of the window at gorgeous countryside. I decided that train travel was the ideal way to go. Coast to coast across America. What made me think of that?

When I got off the train at Ardgay, the boys were there waiting for me.

'We thought you might be on this train,' said Phil.

'And guess what we've got?' said Mike.

They had our bicycles. They had gone back up Strathcarron and rescued them from behind the dyke. The machines were not much the worse for having been out for a couple of days, a little damp, but that could soon be fixed, said Phil. And they had also brought back my broom-head.

'Well!' I stood there smiling at them, a bit loon-like. They had taken me by surprise.

'And what's more,' said Phil, 'we bought some grub! We thought we'd go for a picnic.'

We cycled up beside the River Shin, on the opposite bank from Carbisdale, with Mike on James's bike, and Phil and me on mine, and picnicked on the shores of Loch

Shin. There wasn't much sun but there was no rain either and it was unbelievably peaceful. We watched the eddying movement of the water and listened to the calling of the birds.

'I sure like this country,' said Phil, lying back with his hands crossed behind his head. 'Reminds me of Canada.'

'Only Canada's a heck of a lot larger,' said Mike. 'You wouldn't want to get lost in the mist in some of the outlying areas there!'

'I'd like to go sometime,' I said.

'You must,' said Phil.

I lay back too. The sky looked vast, and there were no high-rise blocks cutting into it. Right now, the thought of Glasgow was not one bit tempting, centre or no centre!

'Maggie,' said Phil, 'we're going to have to move on tomorrow.'

I did not speak for a moment, then I said, 'Suppose you'll have to.'

'We've not got all that long left before we fly home,' said Mike. 'And we want to get up to John O'Groats and down the West Coast.'

'Don't suppose you could come with us?' said Phil.

I was tempted, oh yes I was tempted! But no, I could not go. There was James. . . .

'Of course,' said Phil.

It was about time I left the hostel too, since you're expected to stay no more than three days at a time and less in the busy season, but the warden had said he wouldn't put me out, not under the circumstances. Besides, the hostel was not absolutely full, probably because the weather had been so bad.

It was strange that I should feel as I did, I thought, as I lay there listening to the call of birds and buzzing of insects. That morning I had felt so in harmony with James, so close to him, and now here I was in harmony with these boys, and wanting to travel on with them. It didn't make sense. Was I being capricious? If I was, it didn't mean I was being fickle towards James. Or to the boys either. I liked them all!

We packed up our picnic, got ready to head back to the hostel. We were quiet now, thinking of tomorrow.

It was a fair run to Carbisdale, which we had constantly in our sight all the way along the Shin, and I was rather glad that it was Phil who was doing the pedalling and not me. I just had to sit there. I told him it was a splendid way to travel!

He laughed. 'Want to change places?'

'Certainly!'

We did for a few yards, and then fell off and lay in a heap laughing.

Why do things have to come to an end? I sat on my bunk when we got back and fumed a little inside myself. It seems to me that when you get something good going it's taken away too easily. You can't have everything, McKinley! My trouble is that I'd like to. Who wouldn't?

Suddenly, I thought of something. Something frightening and terrible. I jumped off the bunk and began to rummage in my rucksack. I hadn't seen my Cairngorm brooch for a couple of days, not since the day we'd set off for Greenyards. It wasn't in my sack. I tipped the jumbled contents on to the floor and looked more thoroughly. Underclothes, clean and dirty, paperback books, pieces of paper, crumpled chocolate wrappers, and other even more revolting objects; but no brooch. It was definitely not there. I searched my sleeping bag, my clothes, every inch of the dormitory, but there was no sign of it.

I went to the wash room, the common room, the dining room, the kitchen. I asked the warden. No, he said, there had been no jewellery of any kind handed in to him.

I had lost Margaret Ross's Cairngorm brooch!

Chapter 9

I had lost the Cairngorm brooch that had belonged to my great-great-granny, Margaret Ross. She had carried it safely from Greenyards across the hills down to Inverness-shire to the glen where she had met her future husband. And I, without a sister to carry on my back, had managed to lose it. I had been wearing it when we set off to Strathcarron that day, I remembered pinning it on my shirt. But I couldn't remember seeing it after that. Of course I'd had other things on my mind. I went back to the dormitory and sat on my bunk. Think, McKinley, think! Had I taken it out when I came home? No, I was pretty sure I hadn't.

I must have lost it somewhere between the hostel and Glencalvie. What an area to look in! How could I possibly hope to search all those miles, over those rutted paths, through the rocks, across the burn, in the church, no, the two churches?

I could have howled with frustration and misery. What would my granny say? She had kept the brooch herself all these years, treasured it, and given it to me only last summer. It was the only heirloom that she would pass on; almost everything else she had owned had been lost when her cottage went on fire last summer.

I trailed downstairs to tell Phil and Mike.

'We'll just have to go and look for it,' said Phil.

'Look for it?' said Mike. 'In Strathcarron and

Glencalvie? You'd need a divining rod!'

'We can't give up until we've tried,' said Phil.

My heart warmed to him. I suppose that he understood how I felt, considering that his great-great-grandfather had beaten out the same kind of trail as my great-great-granny. We had this bond, of our ancestors coming from a common glen, of being evicted Rosses, and I knew that if possible Phil would help me find the brooch.

'Let's eat,' said Phil, 'and then we'll go take a look. It's light till late after all.'

We ate. Mike eyed us apprehensively. I didn't think it was fair that he should have to make the trip again since he had no ancestors and had had to go once already. I said so. Phil agreed.

'I know when I'm not wanted,' said Mike with a grin. 'You don't have to twist my arm!'

Phil and I took the bicycles and set off on our second trip up Strathcarron.

As we rode we kept our eyes glued to the ground. We were looking for a glint of yellow amber. I thought it would be no easier than the needle in the haystack carry-on. Phil was optimistic; he said it was often surprising how often, when one did go back to look for something, one found it. At least that had been his experience in life. It might have been his experience but I couldn't say the same. I seem to have the knack of losing things completely. My mother claims I'd lose my head if it wasn't tied on.

We passed Wester Gruinards and stopped a little way along. Leaving the bikes at the side of the road, we retraced our steps to the cottage of Margaret Ross. It was very quiet, in the way that evening in the country often is, and even the sheep were making little sound. I love the feeling of evening stillness, it always gets to me more than any other time of day, and as we stood there looking across the Carron to the hills, I almost forgot what we were here for. We stood for a few minutes listening to the call of a bird and the lap of the water before Phil said, 'Come on then, Maggie! We're going to make a real good search.'

We searched thoroughly amongst the weeds and fallen rocks, inside and outside the cottage, but had no luck.

'We've still plenty to go,' said Phil, gazing further up the glen.

He was dead right there. Miles. The sun was lowering into the western sky, sending flushes of hot pink through the leaden grey clouds. We returned to the bicycles, continued along the road, and after a bit came to the Free Presbyterian Church. Again, we dismounted, went into the church and saw that the same silver coins sat on the white cloth on the table inside the porch. No one appeared to have been there in our absence; as far as I could see, there was no evidence that anyone ever came there. Perhaps those coins lay from one year's end to the next.

There was no brooch there either. And no crannies in this building for it to lurk among. I felt it was fated.

'Nonsense!' said Phil. 'I don't believe in things being fated. Not like that anyway. Not brooches.'

'Maybe it was destined to be returned to its original glen?'

'Destined nothing! The brooch is going to go back to Glasgow with you.'

Our next stop was the Presbyterian Church at Croick. It felt odd going back, remembering how we had crawled in in the dead of night and slept on the floor. Phil had a torch with him. He shone it up and down the pews, round the floor, into the corners, and then we went out into the graveyard and searched between the stones. We read the names as we passed. Many Rosses. Mary Ross. Dolina Ross. David Ross – Taxman of Craigs, died 1865. So he had not left after the Clearances. And now a Margaret Ross who had died in 1912. We thought of all those people who had lived and died in the glen.

'All related to us in some kind of way I guess?' said Phil. I nodded.

'Well, I dunno!' He scratched his head. 'That brooch of yours. . . . We *could* go up Glencalvie I suppose, but—'

'Oh we can't do that.' It was starting to get dark.

'I'm real sorry, Maggie.'

'Thanks anyway, Phil.'

On impulse, I put out my hand to him. He took it, and held on to it. We looked at one another for a moment, during which I felt a strange shiver of excitement; then, in the next instant, we were in one another's arms, and he was kissing me, and I was kissing him, and I felt as I had never done with James, or any other boy. I felt – what did I feel? I wasn't sure exactly, was only aware that I was in a turmoil, and nothing else existed beyond Phil and myself. How could I be like this with him? I hadn't known him so very long. It didn't make sense. But all this had nothing to do with sense. It was an area beyond all boundaries I'd ever known. I had certainly never been there with James.

'James,' I cried, pulling myself away from Phil.

He let me go. He half-closed his eyes, shook his head. 'Sorry,' he muttered. 'I was forgetting.'

Standing apart, we did not look at one another's faces, but every bit of me knew that he was there. We were quiet. I realised that I was trembling, and my heart was racing so madly that I had to put a hand over it to steady it.

Phil sighed. 'Guess we'd better go.' He came to me, put his hands round the side of my face, tilting it a little so that I had to look into his eyes. I could hardly bear it. 'I didn't mean to upset you, Maggie.'

I could say nothing. He kissed me very softly on the forehead. My legs were weak as I climbed on to the bicycle. We said very little on the journey back; we rode side by side down the darkening glen, repassing all the now familiar landmarks. I would have been happy to have ridden on into the night – I, Maggie McKinley, who hated cycling – and never to have reached Carbisdale.

Mike met us in the porch saying that there had been a telephone call for me from Mrs Fraser. She had left no message.

'Where did you say I was?'

'I told her you'd gone out on your bike with my pal.'

I groaned. Mrs Fraser would be pleased to hear that, and would probably pass on the information to James. I wondered what she'd wanted, but no doubt I would hear in the morning.

We had a little time in the common room before bed.

'Would you like to see my stones?' asked Phil. He had been collecting them on his way round the British Isles.

'Him and his stones!' groaned Mike. 'Wherever we go we're laden down like pack mules.'

I said that I would, so Phil brought a pile down and spread them on the floor. The colours were beautiful, greys, pinks, slatey-blues, purple, mauve, and I was fascinated to hear him talk about them. And all the time he crouched beside me, I was conscious of his body close to mine. Once, when our hands touched accidentally, he glanced up at me, then quickly looked away. Even that brief touch set me tingling again, made my face flush with heat.

Eleven o'clock came too quickly. I would have liked to have stayed up all night, to have walked till dawn. I was as restless as a grasshopper.

'See you in the morning!' we said.

I tossed and turned all night.

The morning was not good.

'We'll give you our addresses,' said Phil, 'and you must give us yours.'

'Yes,' I said.

We sat on at the breakfast table over the dirty dishes, not saying much, elbows on the table, staring at one another. I wanted to say, 'Stay!' Would he if I had? I didn't say it.

Phil and I washed the dishes, whilst Mike went off upstairs to pack. Afterwards, we wandered out on to the terrace and looked down at the river.

'It's been very nice, Maggie,' said Phil, hesitantly. 'These last few days.'

'Yes,' I said. 'It has. Very nice.'

It didn't seem much to say but, on the other hand, what else could I have said? What could he have said? I hate goodbyes, am no good at them. A goods' train passed down below, going north, probably up to Wick and Thurso, where Phil and Mike were heading. I wished I was going with them. Then I remembered James, and of course I didn't wish it any more. Or did I? I was torn, confused. Why is anything never straightforward?

We went back into the hostel to find Mike in the hall with the rucksacks at his feet, looking at a map. I felt again a great urge to get back on the road, to move, to travel north. We exchanged addresses.

Phil opened his mouth. I thought he was going to say something. I waited. He didn't say it.

'Right?' asked Mike.

'Right,' said Phil.

They shouldered their rucksacks. I walked with them down the drive as far as the gate, and there we shook hands, kind of awkwardly.

'Have a good trip,' I said.

Phil nodded. 'See you, Maggie!'

I turned away, not wanting to watch them go. Stupid

fool McKinley! A few yards up the drive, I did turn and looked back to wave.

'Goodbye,' I called. 'Goodbye.'

I went slowly the rest of the way up the drive. So that was that. And now I must be thinking of getting to Golspie to see James.

When I arrived at the hospital, I discovered that he had been discharged! They had needed his bed urgently. The nurse said she thought his parents had taken him to their hotel.

I ran to the hotel and saw with relief that the Frasers' car was still parked outside.

They were all three in the lounge reading magazines about country life.

'How are you, James?' I asked.

'Fine.'

'That's what *you* think,' said his mother. 'I expect you'll find later that you're not as strong as you think you are.'

'Now, Mother!' said James.

Mrs Fraser had a plan. She and Mr intended to stay in the north for a few days, now that they were here, and she saw no reason why we shouldn't all continue our holiday together. It would be much nicer for us to travel by car, and she would be able to keep an eye on James and see that he was all right.

'You can still stay in your hostels. You don't have to stay in hotels with us.'

It was a difficult thing to argue against under the circumstances, but the thought of travelling for the rest of the fortnight with Mrs Frazer made my heart sink to zero. I scratched my elbow. Everything seemed to be going wrong. I had lost my granny's Cairngorm brooch, Phil and Mike had gone, and now here we were landed with Mr and Mrs Fraser.

We had afternoon tea, and Mrs Fraser talked. She

thought that it would be a good idea to move on tomorrow, and that we might as well continue up the east coast to Caithness. I cheered up a little; there might even be a possibility that we would encounter Phil and Mike at John O'Groats. Forget Phil! I gave myself a little silent lecture.

After lunch, we went for a run in the car. Suffering doughnuts! I hadn't come all this way to go for nice runs in a car. Then I shook myself, gave myself another dressing down. You're being dead selfish, McKinley, think of James, how he must feel, with his sore head and aching ribs, because I felt sure they must be aching even though he would not admit it. I'm not all that good at coping with disappointments. It's about time I learned, isn't it, Granny?

The countryside was lovely though, so I did enjoy that. We stopped and went for a short walk in a forest. The pines smelled delicious, soaring high above our heads, and I suppose one thing about the amount of rain we'd been having was that it did bring the smells out. It was a very clean, fresh, sweet world. Yes, even with all the tribulations.

'Sh!' said Mr Fraser, holding out his hand.

We froze, like statues. In front of us, in a little clearing, stood three red deer. They were just standing there, heads raised as if trying to catch any sounds on the air. We held our breaths. After a few seconds they must have felt our presence for they made one turn in our direction, then quickly and gracefully galloped off out of sight. It helped make my afternoon.

In the evening I ate with the Frasers, and then Mr ran me back to Carbisdale. That was the part I didn't like very much, the arriving back, for the hostel, although it was full of all sorts of people, seemed lonely. I went hopefully into the common room looking around, thinking that perhaps, who knows, Phil and Mike might have changed their minds, or not got a lift? But there was no sign of the sandy head or the black one. They were probably at John O'Groats by this time, making friends with new people. By tomorrow they would have half forgotten me. I would be that wee girl from Glasgow that they'd met further back in their holiday. What was her name now? Quit feeling sorry for yourself, McKinley!

I went up to bed.

Chapter 10

Poor Mrs Fraser's plans came to nothing, for early in the morning of the day we were due to set off north, she had a telephone call from Grandfather Fraser in Edinburgh that sent her zooming off immediately southwards. James came to the hostel to tell me.

'Catriona's had a miscarriage.'

'*What*?'

'She's lost the baby.'

My first thought was, well, perhaps it might be for the best, and then I realised that of course Catriona would be suffering like mad. It had happened when they were in Minorca, but they were flying home that day.

The Frasers were sitting outside in their car. Mrs looked as pale as she had at Catriona's wedding. James was to stay here. I promised his mother I would see that he was sensible, didn't overtax himself, etc., but although she had to extract the promises I could see that her concern had shifted from James to Catriona.

So we were alone again, James and I, due to Catriona's misfortune. The warden let James check in for one night. We talked about Catriona all morning, and when I did say that perhaps it might be a good thing in the long run James rounded on me furiously, saying I was hard-hearted.

'I'm only being realistic. It wouldn't have been very convenient for Catriona to have a baby at seventeen.'

'You can't judge these things by how convenient they are.'

'No, maybe not,' I conceded, though not with much conviction. 'But it's not *just* a case of convenience after all. It would have changed her life.'

James said that we shouldn't be afraid of things that change our lives.

'Great! You talk about things changing your life but that's only if it suits you. You wouldn't like your life changed, not really drastically, would you?'

'But things like marriage and having a family—'

I didn't want to discuss things like getting married and having a family so I cut across him saying, 'Let's leave that hoary old topic. Let's enjoy ourselves.'

Since James was well below par, in spite of what he said, there wasn't a great deal that we could do except idle around in the area. This we did happily enough, picking bunches of wild flowers, stopping to smell the honeysuckle and wild roses. And all the time I had my eyes open in case I should see the gleam of my Cairngorm brooch in the road. James was sympathetic, when I told him.

'What a shame, Maggie!'

Yes, it certainly was a shame. Mine.

We went to Ardgay and bought postcards in a little shop and sat on a stone outside to write them. When it comes to writing postcards I'm nowhere. James wrote his quickly, covering them with his neat handwriting. What was he telling them? Was he recounting the tale of his night in Glencalvie? The trouble is it seems to me, when it comes to postcards, that there's either too much or too little to say.

To my granny I wrote, 'Found Greenyards.' And then lost the Cairngorm brooch? How could I write that? That wouldn't bring much pleasure to the old soul. I contemplated the hills across the valley watching the light move on them, changing from grey to misty-blue to violet.

'Haven't you even written one yet?' asked James. He had six in his hand and was putting his pen away in his pocket. I returned to Granny's postcard. Greenyards. What would she like to know about it? 'It looked very green and peaceful,' I wrote, 'James sends his love, as do I.' That would do.

To my parents and family I wrote, 'Dear McKinleys, I hope you are keeping the drains unblocked and the loos flushing. James sends his love to all the family females. Your one-and-only Maggie.' One's enough! I could hear my mother saying that. And that was enough writing for now. My duty was done. Tomorrow I should send a card to Mr Farquharson and Mrs Clark. They probably weren't snowed under with mail every morning and even a picture postcard might cheer their day.

'It's a pity we can't go up to Greenyards and look for it,' said James, 'but it'd be too far for me to walk, I'm afraid.' And his parents had removed the bicycles, making sure that he would not use his. We had promised to travel by public transport; James had been given the money.

He rang home in the evening. I waited on the terrace for him, watching the hills and trees, thinking, not so much of Catriona at that moment, but of Margaret Ross. She must have been steeped in this whole landscape, in this misty fresh weather, and the smell of pines and the sight of hills. Perhaps she had gathered wild flowers too, or had life been too hard to bother with such frivolities? No, I supposed life would never be so hard that girls wouldn't pick wild flowers from the hedgerows.

When James joined me he said that Catriona seemed not too bad; it was his mother who was in a worse state. She had sounded very distraught. No doubt, the thought had crossed her mind, as it had mine, that Catriona need not have married after all.

'And Alexander?' I asked. 'How's Alexander?' Nobody seemed to have given him a thought, not even me, until now.

James looked surprised for a moment, as if he couldn't quite remember who Alexander was.

'I don't know. I didn't ask.'

And presumably his mother had not said. Alexander must be hanging around in the background of Heriot Row not knowing what to do with himself, feeling miserable, spurned by Catriona's family, and perhaps, even by Catriona herself?

I was glad I was well away from all that emotional high drama. It's not much in my line. I knew it was not a noble sentiment to have, considering Catriona's troubles, but I sure as heck had it. Those areas of upheaval depress me. James would have said I was afraid of them if I'd voiced my thoughts aloud. He often accused me of burying my head in the sand if something was unpleasant. Could be true. I'm not denying it particularly, nor trying to pretend it's even admirable. But at my age it seemed to me that I didn't have to be too concerned about those matters. On the other hand, there was Catriona, who was my age, being involved. That would have been one of James's lines. It was really funny, for James was standing beside me looking at the hills, and there was I having a little chat with him in my head when I could have been talking to him in person. It's often safer to chat in your head to somebody.

Safety? Was that what I wanted? What a horrible thought! It didn't appeal to me very much, in theory, but I supposed in some areas that was what I did want. Yet, on the other hand, I could be pretty rash at times. I seemed to veer between the two.

The next day, we moved on. The train took us north,

through glorious countryside, often running close to the sea, as far as Helmsdale where there was a hostel. We were now in Caithness.

There was no room at the hostel! It was a smallish one with only thirty-eight beds, and all were booked. What would we do now? Go on to John O'Groats, I suggested, but James said it was too late in the day to move on, and we might not get in there either. The only thing for it was to find a bed-and-breakfast place.

We found one after several tries. It was a small cottage, with lace screens and heavy brown curtains not properly pulled back from the edges of the window, so that the inside was gloomy. It smelt as if the windows hadn't been opened for fifty years. The widow woman who ran it eyed us with suspicion. It was the Sabbath and she did not usually like to take in visitors on the Sabbath. But if she did we must expect no meals for she would not cook on the Lord's Day. I was about to say to James, 'Let's go' – I would have preferred a barn – when she decided to take us. Presumably, she wanted the money.

She showed us into our rooms, one on either side of the passage. The smell in mine was as stale as an old clothes shop. When she went out I wrestled with the window but it was stuck fast.

We went out into the town to look for food, and before we went she cautioned us that we must be in before ten o'clock, for she would lock the door then. She seemed to disapprove of us going out at all. Did she think we should starve just because it was Sunday?

It was a beautiful evening, dead calm. I didn't like Caithness nearly as much as Sutherland because it's very flat, but the light is fantastic, especially over the sea. We sat on the cliffs and watched it. To begin with, the sea was almost the colour of milk, soft and bluey-white, then gradually it took on all the colours of the sky: pale turquoise, yellow, pink, orange, mauve, purple. I had never seen sea like it in my life before.

The widow woman was waiting for us when we came in. She stood in the passage and watched James and I go to our separate abodes. I wondered if she'd keep up an all-night vigil. In a way I was pleased to think of her there, on guard, for James had had that intense look in his eyes again when we'd been sitting on the cliffs. In my usual cowardly way, I preferred to avoid a confrontation if possible. I was glad now that we had not settled for a barn.

Breakfast was served in the woman's living room. Porridge and kippers. I didn't mind that but hated the feeling of eating in someone else's house, a stranger's. And she was hovering in the doorway as if she thought we might steal her silver. Who would want it I couldn't imagine! It was greenish, and my fork smelt.

'Will you be staying another night?' she asked.

James said we were not sure. I tried to signal to him, indicating definitely not, but he paid no attention. We were lucky to have anywhere to stay at this time of the year, he informed me. The widow woman said she must know by twelve, she would hold the rooms no longer. You would have thought she was doing us a favour, but the price she was charging wasn't chicken-feed. James, however, was paying, so I couldn't complain about that.

We returned to the hostel in case of a cancellation. There was none.

'Why don't we go on to John O'Groats?' I was beginning to feel like a gramophone record. James said that he did not feel like it particularly – I had a good idea why not – and would prefer to explore around here. The district was rich in prehistoric remains. And we could go to Kildonan which had been the scene of a gold rush in 1868.

He got his way, and the widow woman had us for

another night. She addressed herself exclusively to James, she seemed to like him, but me she did not approve of. I didn't lose any sleep over it. Any that I did lose was because I was cold: there weren't enough blankets on the bed.

Over porridge and kippers, second time round, I told James I absolutely refused to spend one more night in this place. It was horrible! I didn't care if she heard me or not.

'Okay! Keep your hair on!'

We paid her, and carried our rucksacks to the station.

'Where to now?' said James.

I did not dare say it.

'Maybe we should head south again?' he said. 'You like Sutherland and Easter Ross better anyway, don't you?'

'All right. Why don't we go back to Carbisdale? We've been away two nights, the warden'll probably let us in if there's room.' And there were two hundred beds so there was a good chance there would be.

I would be able to go back to Greenyards again!

My heart lightened as the train approached Bonar Bridge. I felt as if I was returning home. My granny's glen was another home to me after Glasgow; perhaps this was going to be yet another. Before I was done I might have homes all over the world. I hoped so. The idea appealed to me.

Thinking of homes, I decided to ring mine, reversing the charges, which made my mother tell me every few seconds that I was phoning long distance, as if I didn't know, and also that it was the peak time of day, which I had forgotten. Well, anyway, how were they all? That was what I wanted to know. They were all fine, more or less, said my mother, and then proceeded to tell me all the things that were wrong with everybody.

Jean had had a tiff with her boyfriend and was moping around like a week of wet Sundays, Aunt Jessie had had her hair re-tinted and it had come out too fiery a red, my father of course had plenty of things wrong with him, but most of all it was worries about the shop. Business was bad. Yes, it was, very bad. And the way this inflation was going. . . . She sighed. And she was not to get her weekend in Blackpool.

Rashly, I told her about Catriona.

'Maggie, you wouldn't—'

'Oh, don't start worrying about that, Mum! That's one thing you don't have to worry about.'

'What about you and James? You're not thinking of getting engaged or anything yet, are you?'

'Certainly not! If I've told you once I've told you—'

'Oh, I ken what you've told me.'

She remembered again about the price of long distance calls so we said cheerio and rang off. It was James's turn to come into the box to call his family. His mother also remarked straight away that he was ringing at the peak time. She said that Catriona was rather pale, which was understandable, and very quiet, which was worrying. What else did they expect from her? They could hardly expect her to be dancing the Highland Fling up and down Queen Street Gardens.

'And how are you and Maggie?'

'Fine. She's with me in the phone box.'

Now I had to have a few words with Mrs Fraser. Patiently, I answered all her questions about James, not even allowing myself to make a face at the wall as I would have done if I had been alone. Mothers! Families!

'We're going to take Catriona up to Inverness-shire for a few days,' said Mrs Fraser. 'Perhaps we'll see you there? I'm sure Catriona would like to see you, Maggie. She was saying this morning that she would.'

I said that we might come back a day or two early so that I would have time to see her.

'Is Alexander coming too?' I asked.

'Alexander? Oh no, he won't be coming. He's got to start work again.'

James took the receiver back for a few minutes. He said yes, his ribs were healing. Yes, his head was improving. No, he was not tiring himself out. Yes, he was doing everything the doctor had said. He winked at me; I grinned back at him.

He rang off. We went out into the cold fresh air. We were always griping about our families but here we were checking in regularly, wanting to talk to them every few days, in spite of what we said. In advance, I knew what my mother would say to me, and yet I had to hear her say it, and each time I spoke to her I felt a teeny bit homesick. I could just see me in my wanderings around the world, in the middle of the Australian Desert, or the Kalahari Bush, going to the nearest outpost to make a telephone call back to Glasgow to speak to me mum!

The road up to Carbisdale Castle was very familiar. I like things to be familiar, to know each bend, to get that feeling of recognition. In fact, I'm not much good with brand-new places, have to have time to get used to them. The castle loomed up above us, beckoning us. We were offered a couple of lifts which we refused, preferring to walk. I was in no hurry now, felt oddly peaceful after the tumult of the last few days, as did James, who smiled at me and took my hand, swinging my arm gently to and fro.

'We'll go to Greenyards tomorrow if you like. I think I can make it.'

'Yes, I would like. I would like that very much!'

There were one or two girls in my dormitory that I'd seen before. We greeted one another like long-lost friends, and I stayed chatting for a while, exchanging notes of what we'd been doing. They had seen Phil and Mike in the hostel at John O'Groats.

'Where were they going?' I asked.

'Along to Tongue and Cape Wrath.'

So they were moving in the opposite direction from us. They had been to the north of Scotland and now were travelling west; we were travelling south and east, and never the twain shall meet.

The next day, James and I picnicked at Greenyards, on the banks of the Carron. We got soaked.

'You wouldn't think it could rain so much and for so long would you?' I said, as we huddled under a tree.

James did not reply. He just stood staring out at the rain, as I did, thinking of the several miles we would have to walk back.

We staggered along, somewhat sodden, and as luck would have it at times like those, were offered no lifts either to decline or accept. James seemed tired, he limped a bit, and I saw that he kept putting his hands to his ribs.

'Are you all right?'

'Fine.'

He would never admit to being anything else, not like me who moans and groans when there's anything wrong. He is of the stiff-upper-lip outward-bound school which doesn't allow you to moan and groan. Our family are moaners and groaners. Too much! It is one of my endless resolutions: to try to moan less. If I'm ever able to adopt all these resolutions, I shall be an absolute saint. And a pain in the neck to anybody who comes near me.

The rain didn't let up.

'In the olden days they must have got soaked repeatedly,' I said. 'I can just imagine Margaret Ross tramping up and down here, with her red shawl over head, and holding her skirts out of the mud.'

James was not interested in Margaret Ross today. I daresay he had had enough of her anyway. Even with the rain bucketing down and beating us about the head, I kept my eyes wide open and cast down, still looking hopefully for my Cairngorm.

'I'll never forgive myself for losing that brooch,' I moaned, quickly forgetting my resolution.

'Well, it's done now,' said James. 'There's no use crying over spilt milk.'

I knew he didn't mean to sound unsympathetic but he was probably at the end of his tether, and there was I groaning about a brooch which I myself had been stupid enough to lose. But I, even knowing that, still felt a bit annoyed with him for sounding so sharp.

He stumbled, falling on to one knee.

'James!' I cried, crouching beside him.

I felt guilty that I had let him come all the way to Greenyards. It seemed a fated place for the two of us. I put my arms round him, full of contrition and misery.

'James, James,' I said softly, and kissed the top of his wet head.

He lifted his head to look at me, with rain running all down his face. I could see now that he was almost done for, not in a total sense, but for that day. He had overtaxed his strength sorely. His mother would have killed me if she could have seen him!

'I can't carry you on my back, I'm afraid.'

That made him laugh. And then I began to laugh too, at the idea of me, an eight-stone weakling, carrying him, a twelve-and-a-half stone hulk, over my shoulder. We sat there in the middle of the wet road laughing, with the rain cascading all over us.

We struggled to our feet, and I put an arm around his waist, in an effort to support him. It was rather a case of the lame leading the lame. Fortunately, two or three miles from the hostel, we did get a lift, which took us to the door of the hostel.

James had to go upstairs immediately and lie down.

After I had changed and hung up my dripping garments in the bathroom, I went down to the kitchen to make a pot of tea and some sandwiches. I was so hungry I could have eaten the soles off my sandals.

I walked into the kitchen, and there, standing by the cooker, were Mike and Phil.

Chapter 11

Phil laughed when he saw my face.

'Hi, Maggie!'

'Where have you come from? I thought you were going to Cape Wrath.'

'We did go to Cape Wrath. We came down the west coast too, as far as Ullapool, and then got a lift in a car that was going to Bonar Bridge. So here we are!'

There they were! And looking just the same, exceedingly familiar, smiling, unfussed. They were the tonic that I needed at that moment, though I wondered if it would be what James would need.

'Want some hamburger and beans?' asked Mike.

They didn't have to ask me twice, they knew that. We ate, and caught up on our news.

'How long are you going to be here for?' I asked.

'Only one night I'm afraid,' said Phil. 'We have to push on tomorrow, down to Prestwick. We fly back to Canada the day after tomorrow.'

I would only have one more evening with them, but that didn't matter, for after not expecting to see them any more, one extra evening was a bonus. I was so pleased to see them that I just sat and grinned at them. Funny, isn't it, the way you take to some people quickly and easily, and with others you could labour on for years and not feel you connect in any way?

We went into the common room, where we carried on

talking, and then, suddenly, I realised that it had gone eight o'clock, and James still hadn't come down. Mike went up to see if he was all right.

'It's real nice to see you again, Maggie,' Phil said, when Mike had gone.

'Nice to see you too.' I felt a blush rising up from my neck and spreading across my cheeks. Stupid fool McKinley! Talk about trying to appear cool and sophisticated, and at ease! I had to look down at my plate, away from those dark, watching eyes across the table.

Mike came back to say that James wasn't getting up, that he felt he needed to rest. I went back upstairs with Mike. James was lying in a bottom bunk looking rather awful. My heart did a loop the loop. Maybe he'd had a real relapse? Should I get a doctor? I suggested it but he turned the idea down flat. *Don't dare!* He said that he was only tired, he had obviously pushed himself a little bit too much, and would be fine in the morning. He didn't want anything to eat, thank you. He sounded cool, but then he *was* ill. I saw that he had Mike fixed in his eye. Mike got the message and vanished.

Kneeling down beside James, I took his hand. 'Are you really all right? I'm worried about you.'

'Are you? You took long enough to come up and see me.'

It was true that I had. I had forgotten. . . . But I shouldn't have forgotten him! I felt irresponsible and inadequate.

'I'm sorry, James.'

He closed his eyes. 'It's all right. You'd better get back to your friends now, hadn't you?'

I scratched my right ankle which seemed to have got bitten by an army of midges. Okay, so he didn't have to sound like that! Get back to *your* friends indeed!

'I'll stay here with you, James.'

117

'I want to sleep.'

I stayed there for a few minutes, not knowing what to do or say. I couldn't stand there haranguing him or trying to make him talk to me, not with him in the state that he was. I wondered too if I should get the warden to call a doctor. James lay with his eyes closed, pretending to sleep. He would be furious with me if I called a doctor and made a fuss, so I thought better not add that to his list of grievances against me tonight.

'James?' I whispered.

He did not answer.

I tiptoed away, back to the common room.

'Everything okay?' asked Phil.

I shrugged. 'Think so.'

We settled down again, and, upstairs, James presumably slept. Whenever I thought of him I felt bothered, but what was I to do?

'Hey, Maggie,' said Phil, 'I got a lot of new stones over on the west coast. Some real beauts.'

'Oh, those stones!' groaned Mike. 'It's not as if he can even take them home with him.'

'Why not?' I asked.

Phil laughed. 'On a plane?'

'Oh yes, I'd forgotten.'

I'd never flown, I told the boys.

'You will when you come to Canada,' said Mike.

'I could never afford it.'

'When you're a student you can get a cheap flight,' said Phil.

'All right,' I said. 'I'll come when I'm a student.'

That was a whole year off yet, but still, it was rather nice to make plans for a year ahead, vague plans though they might be.

'Would you like to see my new stones?'

'She wouldn't dare say no,' said Mike.

Phil went upstairs and returned with his arms full.

'The west coast was really great for stones on the beaches. There was one spot over near a place called Achiltibuie. I could've spent the day there just picking up the whole beach.'

'You don't have to tell me!' said Mike. 'Think I'll go make us some coffee.'

Off he went, and Phil showed me the latest additions to his collection.

'It's going to be real hard having to dump them somewhere. But it would be a bit much having to pay excess baggage on this lot.'

We laughed at the idea of Phil staggering on to the plane laden down with an enormous bag of stones.

'I'd like to take them,' I said. 'Well, some at least. One or two. A few. I tell you what, Phil, I'll keep them for you.'

I rather liked that idea, of keeping something for a friend, and that way keeping something of him too.

'Would you really? That would be great.'

He put some large, smooth, cool stones into my hands. A pink one, then a mauve, then a greenish-grey. He frowned, pondering over his collection, trying to decide which to save.

'Some rose-coloured quartz I think. And here's a piece of sunstone. Can you take any more, Maggie?'

'Of course. Of course!' At that moment I felt capable of taking not only all these stones, but all the others he had collected before as well. I was in one of those expansive moods when I would have agreed to anything.

'Here's an absolute beaut. Look at the veins in it, Maggie! You should have seen it wet from the sea. They should all be polished, then they would gleam.'

I would polish them; I'd learn.

'And here's a little bit of agate.'

'It's gorgeous. They all are, Phil.'

'Next time I come to Scotland—' He stopped. Was he going to have said, 'I'll take you looking for stones too,' and then thought of James? I would never know, for Mike arrived carrying three cups of coffee.

By the time Phil had finished I had a pile of stones in front of me, stacked like a pyramid.

'Are you sure you want to be bothered with all that clobber, Maggie?' asked Phil. 'It seems kinda much to load you up with?'

'I don't mind. No, really!'

'Don't tell me you're going to take all that rubbish with you, Maggie?' said Mike.

'Why not? I think they're gorgeous.'

'Crazy!' said Mike.

We drank our coffee. We were happy. And I did not allow myself to think that there would not be another evening with the boys for a long, long time. Nor did I allow myself to think too much about James. Every now and then either Mike or Phil slipped upstairs to check on him. Each time they went he was sleeping, or they thought that he was, and that as far as they could tell his sleep was peaceful. He had probably just overdone it this afternoon, that was all. That was enough of course, and it was lying on my conscience. My conscience seemed to be in the habit of getting over-burdened. Sometimes I wished it would lie down and sleep for a while.

Before bed, we went for a short walk. I walked between them, linking arms with theirs. We went down the drive into the quiet country road, smelling the hedgerows, hearing the night move quietly above and around us. And as usual with nightfall, the smells seemed to be even better.

Phil sighed. 'I wish we didn't have to go back tomorrow. I could just stay here forever.'

That was the way the north of Scotland seemed to get

you: it made you want to stay on and on. The thought of the town was not appealing, though I knew myself too well not to know that if I did stay here for several months I would end by being bored and mad for the sight of city lights and noise. But, out there on that evening, I did have the feeling of time going on and on and not being pressed in any way. Also, I felt that all this would happen again. I don't know why. It may have been what I wanted to feel.

That night I dreamt, and all my dreams were of Margaret Ross in Greenyards. She was wearing a long tweed skirt, dressed as I imagined one would in the middle of the nineteenth century, and I saw her plainly tramping across the green fields to the river, calling to someone. The image shifted and I saw her carrying her sister on her back. It was night-time, and she was stumbling and falling. Then I realised that Margaret Ross was me – you know the way things happen like that in dreams, when you think it's one person and it suddenly becomes another? The other thing I realised was that it was not Agnes she had on her back; it was James. At that moment I woke.

I was aware that I had been carrying James in my dream. That was ridiculous: he would never need me to carry him, it was more likely to be the other way round. What did it mean? I was too drowsy to think so closed my eyes and let myself drift off again. Again I dreamt of Margaret Ross, and this time she was wearing the brooch, only it was enormous, ten times bigger than in real life. I was sweating in that dream. Now I didn't know if it was I or Margaret Ross who wore the brooch. I could see the brooch in close-up. It turned into a stone, one of Phil's, pink and green-veined, smooth and beautiful. I reached out my hand to touch the pebble; then, as luck would have it, I surfaced.

Eventually, I felt I would sleep no more, I was too restless. I got dressed and tiptoed down through the sleeping hostel and unlocked the front door. The morning had that early, fresh, unused feeling that is really terrific once you brave leaving your bed to go out into it. It's only rarely that I experience it. I'm known to be a real sleepy-head in the mornings, but when I do get up early I think it's absolutely great and resolve to do it more often. Yes, well. . . .

I went a little way down the road. Dew was sitting on the grass and hedges, making them look all pearly. As I walked I was thinking about this place, this area, and its past, and how people were linked in lines stretching out in every direction. It's very comforting to think of threads joining people, even when *they* don't know about it. I was glad of my thread taking me back to Margaret Ross in the eighteen-fifties in Greenyards, and I reckoned that Phil was pretty glad of his link taking him back to his great-great-grandfather in Glencalvie. And then, Phil and I had a link joining us because of them.

That morning I was first in the kitchen. A new record for me! Mike came in whilst I was frying bacon.

'You up already?'

'I've been up for hours!'

'So has Phil.'

'Phil? Where is he?'

'Search me! He went out ages ago, hasn't come back yet.'

Mike also told me he'd seen James, and that he looked much better.

So Phil had also felt restless this morning and wanted to have a last look round! I wished that I might have met him, we could have gone together. In fact, I felt cheated now that I knew he had been about at the same time.

Mike and I were in the middle of breakfast when Phil

appeared. He had his hands in the pockets of his anorak, and he was grinning.

'What have you got to be so pleased about?' asked Mike.

Phil pulled up a chair and sat down beside me. He looked rather like the cat who had pinched the cream off the doorstep.

'You'll never guess what I found this morning?'

I stared at him. He couldn't. . . . 'Not –' I couldn't get it out.

He nodded. 'Your brooch, Maggie. I found your brooch!'

'But how? Where?'

He'd started thinking about it when he'd gone to bed the night before, had tried to imagine all the most likely places where I might have lost it. And then he'd remembered that I'd fallen off my bike.

'I thought there was a chance you might have lost it then. So I got up early and went to take a look. I raked around in the undergrowth and – ' He put his hand into his pocket ' – I found it!' He brought out his hand, and there on the palm lay my great-great-granny's Cairngorm brooch.

'Phil!' I jumped up and flung my arms around his neck. I could hardly believe it. Then I realised what I was doing, got a bit embarrassed, and had to sit down. Phil was still grinning.

The brooch was unharmed, and as lovely as ever. I felt dazed with relief to have it back in my possession.

'I'm *so* pleased. You've no idea!'

'I think I have. As a matter of fact I'm kinda pleased too.'

I pinned the brooch back on to my shirt, making sure that the catch was securely fastened. It seemed like an omen that Phil had found it. I'm not sure whether I believe in omens or not, but once, when I was discussing them with Mr Scott, he said that an omen might have meaning if you gave it one. I decided that maybe this was an omen I wanted to give meaning to. And the meaning I took from it? That I would see Phil again.

James walked in.

'James!' In my nervousness I dropped my cup and broke it. Phil and I dived underneath the table to pick up the pieces, knocking knees together in the process.

I came up, conscious that my face was probably as red as it was capable of getting, considering the dun colour it is normally. My finger was bleeding slightly. I sucked it. I felt guilty again, without quite knowing why. Except that I had been neglecting James. No, I'd more than neglected him; I'd forgotten him.

'You look a heck of a lot better this morning, James,' said Phil.

James said that he was fine, just fine. His voice was clipped. He sat down beside us and I jumped up to cook his breakfast although he protested that he could do it himself.

I was glad to escape to the kitchen and busy myself with the mundane task of frying bacon and egg. My tummy seemed to be flipping around rather a lot. I broke the egg, naturally! What was happening to me? I still did care for James a great deal, so why should I be bothered whether I saw Phil again or not?

James and I were both quiet as he ate his breakfast, whilst Phil and Mike chatted. And then the boys went off to pack. James and I sat together saying nothing, until I decided I'd better try apologising. It was becoming a habit.

'I'm sorry, James.'

'For what?'

I shrugged. 'Nothing really.'

'Then why apologise?'

'I don't know—'

'Unless you have something to feel guilty about?'

'I don't. It's just that you're so damned jealous—'

'You over-estimate yourself, Maggie.'

It was idiotic and ridiculous. We were like a couple of kids, sparring, snarling at one another, full of bile and resentment. I got up and left the table. The boys were coming down the stairs, laden-up, ready for the road.

This time I did not go down the road with them, I said goodbye on the porch. It really *was* goodbye this time, there was no hope that we would have any further chance encounters on this journey.

'See you in Canada, Maggie!'

'Yeh, see you!'

Turning away quickly, I went back to James. I had to make things right with him, I couldn't waste everything.

'Let's be friends, James.'

'I don't know if I'm interested, Maggie. You're so selfish—'

'*I* selfish? You're so possessive.'

He stood up. 'I'm nothing of the kind. And to prove it, I'll show you that you don't have to bother about me at all.'

'Are you trying to say you want to finish it between us?'

'Exactly that.'

'Okay, if that's the way you want it.'

'I think that's the way *you* want it.'

'I've never said I wanted it that way.'

'You didn't have to say, it was pretty obvious.'

Yappity-yap, and so we went on. We were like two dogs with our teeth in a bone. We growled and hissed at one another, until, in the end, I blew my top totally. I told him he was a pain in the neck, I never wanted to set eyes on him again. I must have been crazy to have spent a year on him, he was unfair, stupid, pompous, boring, and a real drag to be with! He told me a few things about myself too, but I, needless to say, refused to listen.

Chapter 12

It was peaceful up Strathcarron. There were no sheriff's men evicting Ross women, and no James bawling me out. I sat inside the shell of Margaret Ross's cottage and stared out at the hills. This peace was what I needed. I needed to be away from everyone for a few hours. I thought that during that time I would be able to think things out but, funnily enough, now that I was on my own, I found that I wasn't thinking much about anything at all. I felt submerged into the landscape.

Later, I went further along the road and over the bridge to the church at Croick. I wandered around the churchyard with the memories of Phil's ancestors in my mind. And memories of Phil and Mike too. They would be moving southwards, making for Prestwick, and home. Home was Canada, a long way away, and I must forget about them in the meantime.

I had left the hostel in such a hurry that I'd brought nothing to eat with me. My tummy was rumbling with hunger which I had to ignore. For once Maggie McKinley was going to do without food rather than return to civilisation. A couple of American visitors came into the church whilst I was there and I gave them a spiel about the Clearances, telling them all about my great-great-granny again. It was good to have someone new to tell the story to. Perhaps I might even get a job as a guide? It would give me a chance to blether on without people complaining.

'It's a cute little church,' said the American, the male one.

He took pictures of the church and the churchyard, and of me. Maggie McKinley amongst the tombs of Croick! I wanted to giggle when I thought of their friends and relatives back home gawping at me on some big screen. I was looking my usual dishevelled self, hair on end, jeans crumpled. My mother and Aunt Jessie would have been real dithered to see me being snapped thus for American posterity.

'Do you live round here, dear?' asked the American female.

'Yes,' I said. Today I did: that was how I felt.

Mercifully, they had some chocolate, which they shared with me. My tummy subsided a little with gratitude.

They went on, I stayed. A few more people came in the course of the afternoon, mostly tourists from abroad, but one or two Scots as well. It was surprising to see so many people there, but the day was half decent, for a change. I guided them round, giving them my talk again. Maggie McKinley the custodian at Croick! In the course of the afternoon I acquired a few sweets, a sandwich and a bottle of Coke. One man even offered me a tip but that I refused, saying, 'Oh no, I never take gratuities.'

I was sitting in a pew in the empty church when another visitor arrived. Sensing a shadow in the doorway, I looked round. There stood James.

'What do *you* want?'

'To talk to you.'

I said that I wasn't at all sure I wished to speak to him.

'Oh stop all that, Maggie. We have to talk.'

I got up. He had come to me quite quickly. Once before, when we'd had a really big row, it had taken him

127

ages to swallow his pride. Of course I hadn't got around to swallowing mine!

'Let's go outside,' he said. 'I don't like it in here, it's too creepy.'

We walked back as far as the bridge and sat on the parapet. I stared down at the burn.

'We must talk sensibly, Maggie. We have to decide if we want to go on together or not.'

There was silence for a moment. I drummed my heels softly against the parapet.

'What do you think then?' he asked. 'Do you want to go on or call it a day?'

I didn't really know what I wanted.

'Say something, Maggie! We can't get anywhere if you don't.'

'I don't know what to say.'

His voice became cooler. 'Presumably then you don't care at all?'

'No, that's not true.'

'So you do care about me?'

'Yes, I suppose so.'

'You suppose so? You don't sound very enthusiastic.'

'Oh I do care, James, really I do.' I turned to look at him.

'I love you, Maggie,' he said quietly, making me go all pulpy inside.

'Why do we quarrel then?'

James said that he thought all people quarrelled in a close relationship. He said that he didn't want to quarrel with me, to say nasty things, to be possessive, but sometimes he couldn't help it, and he admitted that he had felt jealous about Phil and Mike. He had wanted to have me to himself and resented them being with us so much.

In a moment we were in one another's arms hugging each other and saying we were sorry, we didn't mean it.

And then we were laughing at one another, and I was almost crying. Not that I, Maggie McKinley, am often given to tears, but it was one of those moments of suspension between laughing and crying.

'You do believe I love you, Maggie? Don't you?'

Yes, yes, I believed him. He didn't have to keep asking me.

'I want us to be together all the time.'

'But we can't be. Not when I'm in Glasgow and you're in Edinburgh.'

'Yes, that's a strain. Remember last winter!'

'But there's nothing we can do about it.'

'There is, Maggie. We could get married.'

I knew that the thought had been in his mind, I had known it since Catriona's wedding, but spoken aloud it shattered me. I drew back from him.

'Get married?'

'Wouldn't you like to?'

'But I have to finish my year at school, James.'

'All right, but why not next year?' He was becoming excited. 'We could get married next summer, Maggie. You'd be ready for Edinburgh University and I'd have done my first year.'

'Wait a minute, James.'

'But why not, Maggie? It would be something to look forward to. You're coming to Edinburgh then anyway.'

'I'm not sure—' I spluttered.

'You're not sure you love me? You said you did.'

'I do, I do. But that doesn't mean—'

'If you really loved me you'd want to marry me.'

I didn't think it was that simple but James was in no mood to be talked to rationally. It was a funny thing but I seemed to be the rational one at that moment and he, who normally is, was excited and much more emotional than me.

'Let me think, James. I feel all confused and mixed up.'

But he wouldn't let me think, he couldn't stop talking. He said my family would be pleased, wouldn't they? That I could not deny, but it wasn't my family who were going to marry him. If he wanted he could marry Aunt Jessie, she'd be delighted, except of course for the fact that she did have a husband already. He told me not to be so flippant, this was serious, and I mustn't resort to my usual way of avoiding things by cracking jokes. His family wouldn't be pleased, I pointed out; his mother would have a fit. James said that his mother would have to get used to it, he was eighteen now and could do what he wanted. And I could get married too whether my family agreed or not.

'Quite a lot of students get married nowadays, Maggie. I had a little money left to me on my eighteenth birthday, I could probably buy a small flat with that, and I know that Grandpa would help us. We could go to university during the day together, study in the evenings. We could be together all the time. Doesn't that sound great?'

'I don't think I'm ready yet for marriage,' I bleated mournfully, sounding like one of those sheep on the hills. 'I don't feel responsible enough.'

'Don't be silly. You're always putting yourself down, and it would be nearly another year anyway. You'd be eighteen by then.'

'You make it sound like eighty. I never wanted to get married before I was thirty. I don't see any point in being married before you're middle-aged.'

'Now, Maggie! You're being flippant again. Why are you so afraid of marriage?'

'I'm not.'

'You like being with me, don't you?'

Yes, I did. And I supposed it would be kind of nice to have a little flat and live together. Most of the time we did enjoy one another's company a lot, we were always able to talk about things, which Catriona and Alexander never seemed to have been able to do, and we laughed and enjoyed the same jokes. Most of the time was as much as anyone could expect: that I knew, and I wasn't asking for the moon. I had no ideals about dream men and all that kind of rubbish, like my sister Jean has.

'You don't have to decide just now. But if you say yes, I'd want to give you an engagement ring. It's a ring that belonged to my grandmother.'

An engagement ring. Could I imagine myself waltzing into school on the first day of term flashing three diamonds on the fourth finger of my left hand? Mr Scott would sit back in his chair and roar with laughter. 'You, Maggie, who's always been telling me that you wouldn't get married if somebody came along offering you ten million pounds?' Well, everybody can change their minds, that's no crime. And, anyway, I wouldn't actually have to wear the ring to school. If I did, I knew what would happen: I would lose it. And everybody from the janitor upwards would be rushing around like mad, saying, 'Have you seen Maggie McKinley's diamonds?'

Maggie McKinley with a diamond ring? It hardly seemed to match the rest of me, the battered jeans, the faded shirt, and the ever-so-casual hair.

'Is it diamonds?'

He laughed. 'Does the idea of the ring tempt you?'

'Diamonds are a girl's best friend,' I sang, almost falling off the parapet. 'Isn't that what they say?'

'It's not diamonds, I'm afraid. Emeralds.'

Emeralds. That was better, I had to admit. I'd never seen myself with diamonds. But emeralds are pretty. James put his arm around my waist.

'Would you like to wear my grandmother's emerald ring, Maggie?'

'I might.'

'Something tells me that you will. I have a feeling about it.' He kissed me. He said he had proposed to me in a very suitable place: at the head of Strathcarron, the seat of my ancestors. That must be a good omen. Omens again! Often conflicting ones.

It was time to start heading back for Carbisdale. We didn't exactly hike along at a spanking rate; we wandered, arm-in-arm, looking at one another rather a lot, talking, laughing. James talked about the kind of flat he could buy, he thought he could afford something similar to the one that Grandpa had bought Catriona, and he said that he was sure, once his mother had got used to the idea, she would enjoy herself enormously helping us to furnish it from the sales.

'Hang on! I haven't said yes yet.'

He smiled. 'But you're going to, aren't you?'

I said I didn't know but thought he wasn't listening, he was so carried away by his own plans. Already, in his mind, we were set up in a little flat in Edinburgh, painting the walls and hanging up curtains. I felt as if I was in a trance. Emerald rings. Engagements. Flats in Edinburgh. Did they really have anything to do with me?

By the time we arrived back at the hostel, James was talking as if we were already engaged.

'Your Aunt Jessie will be pleased, won't she?' He grinned. 'Maybe you should ring up your folks tonight.'

Oh no, not tonight! My knees felt weak. And my head was giddy. Of course I had eaten very little all day and I am not much use when deprived of food.

'I'm starving, James.'

'What a girl you are, Maggie! You'd think of your tummy if you were going up the aisle.'

The thought of going up an aisle made me feel even weaker. I tottered into the kitchen where I threw some

132

tinned beans into a pot and turned up the gas to high. I ate the beans neat, some cold, some burnt, without any accompaniment, with James watching me with amusement. A couple of cups of coffee, and my balance was at least partially restored. Now I felt in better fettle to cook the evening meal.

'I can see we'll need to keep our store cupboard well stocked up. I expect we can get quite a good fridge second-hand. Mother's marvellous when it comes to going to sales.'

I opened a tin of stew. It looked revolting, a bit like dog food. On top of it I poured the rest of the beans and stirred the whole lot round together into a great gluey mess.

'We might even manage to get a second hand washing machine. Though I suppose we can always go to the launderette.'

Fridges. Washing machines. Store cupboards. Were they going to become important elements in my life?

'We could get married in July, Maggie, when you finish school. Then we could have the whole summer as a honeymoon.'

'Take it easy, James, please.' My head was aching. I put the mixture on to our plates and stared at it. I felt not at all hungry. 'I need time to get used to the idea.'

'Yes, I know what you're like, Maggie. Anything new throws you at first, doesn't it?'

That irritated me but I didn't show it. I don't like people to claim to know me, to feel they can anticipate how I will react. So maybe I don't like new ideas at first! But this was one pretty enormous new idea. I ate a bit of the bean stew, then pushed my plate away. I leant my elbows on the table and my head on my hands. James talked on, not seeming to be aware that I wasn't eating or talking. He was in excellent spirits. He thought we should move on south tomorrow, and then perhaps the next day go back to the glen in Inverness-shire. I had a horrible feeling that he wanted to get home and break the news of our intending engagement to his family.

I went to bed early, pleading a headache. James was full of concern for me, as he always was. I knew that as a husband he would be attentive and considerate. No one else was in the dormitory so I was able to lie in the quiet room and let myself subside.

I didn't know what I wanted and found I couldn't even think about it. My granny says when you don't know what to do it's best to do nothing. That was what I decided to do that night. I went to sleep, and if I dreamt I did not remember what the dreams were.

We checked out of the hostel in the morning. James lifted my rucksack before I could stop him.

'What on earth have you got in there?'

'Only a few stones.'

'Stones?'

'Just one or two rather pretty ones that I fancied.'

'Don't be crazy, Maggie. You can't carry that load.'

'I can.'

'You'll have to take some of them out, you'll break your back, or I will, carrying it for you.' He didn't have to carry it, I protested. I would carry it myself. He started to ask where I had got all the stones from, then stopped, remembering Phil, I suppose. His mouth changed, becoming harder. He said nothing more but allowed me to pick up the rucksack and put it on my own back. I thought I would collapse under the weight of it.

'Don't let's quarrel, James!'

'I don't want to quarrel, Maggie. But be a sensible girl and take some of the stones out.'

It was a terrible decision to be faced with. I wanted to keep the stones, yet I knew that for James it was not just simply a matter of me shedding some of the load in my rucksack, that it went beyond that. It had to do with Phil, and being committed to James himself.

I let the rucksack slide to the ground, then knelt down and unbuckled the strap. James bent to help.

'It's all right, I can manage.'

I lifted out the stones one by one and laid them at the side of the road, a little bit back, so that they wouldn't be run over. Pink, grey, blue, mauve, soft rainbow colours, lying at the side of the road. I kept three big smooth flat round ones, and the little bit of agate.

'It's only sensible, Maggie. You'd have broken your back in two by the time we'd got to the station.'

I didn't enjoy being sensible. Again, I was wanting life every way. I wanted to have James but to keep Phil's stones too. And apparently, that was too much to ask for. I rearranged the stones, putting them into a little pile, like a cairn. I might come back one day and find that they were still there.

'Come on then, Maggie,' said James breezily. 'Let's get on our way.'

He whistled as we walked down the road to Ardgay. I felt quiet inside, and was wishing that we weren't leaving Easter Ross and my great-great-granny's territory.

If Phil wrote and then I was to write back, I would not tell him about leaving the stones by the wayside. But if Phil wrote, should I write back?

'It's been a funny holiday, hasn't it?' said James. 'I mean, it's not turned out at all as we thought.'

You could say that again! I noticed that James had spoken as if our holiday was over, whereas we could have another two or three days together before going back.

'Where shall we go?' he asked, as we went to buy our tickets.

'Thurso.'

'Don't be daft. Thurso's north.'

'I feel like going north.'

'Another time. Not now, Maggie. We have to go south.'

'London then.'

'Now, Maggie! I think we might as well go to Inverness.'

Inverness. That virtually meant home. I raised no objection. Now I too was beginning to feel we might as well get back.

So the train took us south, to Inverness.

'Well,' said James, when we alighted, 'what now?'

'What do you want to do?'

'Do you think we might just as well go home?'

'If you like.'

At least now I'd have some time with my granny before I went back to Glasgow.

We decided to hitch. Or rather, it might be better to say that I decided, and James agreed. His mother would never know, I told him, we could tell her we got the bus. We got a lift with a nice man in a cement lorry who was going right down to Edinburgh. We rode beside him in the cab, with me in the middle, half sitting on the hot engine. I chatted away to him. He seemed glad of the company.

He deposited us in the town where my granny lives, right in the middle of the village street, just as Mr and Mrs Fraser were coming out of the chemist's shop.

Chapter 13

We jumped on to the kerb, the driver handed down our rucksacks.

'See you again. I'll keep my eyes skinned for you on the road.'

'Thanks a lot,' we said, and then turned to face James's parents.

Mrs Fraser said, 'You didn't have to hitch-hike. I did give you enough money for the bus, James.'

'Oh, Mother!'

I wanted to laugh, for there was James thinking of getting married and his mother was still nagging at him as if he was a small boy. But perhaps our mothers would continue to nag long after we were all married. Thinking of that, I pulled James aside, and hissed in his ear that he was *not* to say anything to his mother and father yet about the prospects of us getting engaged.

'Why not?'

'Because I haven't made up my mind yet.'

He looked surprised.

'We'll talk about it later. We can't stand here whispering. Your mother's already wondering what we're up to.'

Mr and Mrs Fraser took James off to the cottage, I went to my granny's. To be honest, I was really rather glad to have a break away from James. When I admitted that to myself I was appalled, for did it mean that I didn't really love him? Not necessarily, I thought; I felt sure it was normal that people needed to get away from one another from time to time and especially at times like this when momentous decisions had to be taken.

Granny was pleased to see me. Not that she showed it by flinging her arms round me and telling me so, or anything like that. Oh no, that was not at all in Granny's line. She said, 'So you're back, lass. I was just thinkin' about you this morning and wonderin' when you'd be turnin' up again. I kent you'd be back all right. You always turn up eh, just like the bad old penny?'

'Now, Gran! I can see it was time I was back to keep you in order.' I gave her a kiss and a hug. She put her old gnarled fingers round my hand and held me tight.

'What was it like then? Up at Greenyards?'

I sat down beside her at the other side of the fire – for in spite of it being August she did have to have a fire on – and told her all about Greenyards and Strathcarron.

We had a good long session peppered by a few interruptions. First of all came Mr Farquharson chapping at the door at teatime and sniffing the air. 'Fine smell that, Mistress,' he said, addressing Granny. He got some food, needless to say. Then Mrs Clark popped in, thrilled to see me, eyes gleaming, wanting to hear all about it. When I offered her a cup of tea she accepted saying, 'That would be simply lovely,' as if I were offering her nectar from the gods. Both neighbours always came in in the same way, with the same greetings. I like that: it makes you feel everything's in its place. All to do with customs and patterns of behaviour. They interest me. Just as well, since I'm going to study social anthropology.

Thinking of that and future careers brought me back to the matter of James again. If I did marry him – *if* – how could I go abroad to study all those far-off peoples as I wanted to do? He would want to be based in Edinburgh.

Clash of interests. Hm. But if you cared for someone. . . .

Sacrifice. I pondered on that, not at all convinced I was cut out for it. Can you see me with my halo shining? I came back to the present.

'And how is James?' Mrs Clark was asking fondly.

All the older women I know are ga-ga about James. I think half of them fancy him themselves.

'He's fine.'

Mrs Clark waited expectantly. That wouldn't do at all, she'd come for more than that. So I told her about his night of agony on the hillside. My tale was full of melodrama, giving full play to swirling mists and lonely rockstrewn glens. I got quite carried away.

'How awful, Maggie! What an experience for poor James.' Mrs Clark's mascara-spiked eyes became a little misty.

Granny was less disturbed by James's ordeal for she had known many people who had been lost for a night on the hills and returned in the morning. It had been a part of her eighty-four years. Whereas Mrs Clark had been brought up in the south, in Edinburgh.

We had the district nurse as well, a brisk little woman with a jolly face who never seemed to feel down. She had a way of bullying Granny that left me gawping with admiration. She was the only person I had ever known who had been able to tell Granny what to do and get away with it. 'Time for your bath now, Mrs McKinley,' she'd say, and off Granny would go, as meek as a lamb. Two of the other pensioners in the block of flats appeared also; they sat by the fire with us for a while, nodding a little, saying the odd word but not speaking much at all. It was the company they liked.

It was a good evening. And when Granny had gone to bed and I lay on the settee I felt cosy and warm. Tomorrow, I would have to go and see Catriona. That was a disaster area that I'd rather avoid. Coward McKinley! But Catriona was a friend so of course I'd go to see her, there was no question about that, but I wasn't looking forward to it.

In the morning, James arrived in his father's car to fetch me. I was pleased to be going back to the glen, and as we drew closer my heart began to beat more quickly. It always did, going back to that place.

Catriona was sitting in a deck chair in the garden, surrounded by blooming roses, lupins and lavender. She looked great. I had expected her to be wan and worn out, with a kind of traumatic air about her.

I squatted by her feet, and James, discreetly, left us. This all-female chin-wag would not be in his line.

'How are you then, Catriona?'

She shrugged. 'Kind of low.'

'I suppose you would be after all that.'

Catriona's voice picked up. 'But the doctor says there's no reason why I shouldn't have another baby straight away.'

'Straight away? Another baby?' I was flabbergasted. 'Do you mean to say you're thinking of trying to have another baby fairly soon?'

Catriona frowned at me. 'Why not?' Her voice had a chink of ice in it.

'Oh I suppose there's no reason why not.' Though I could think of millions. 'But, Catriona why don't you and Alexander have a little time on your own? Get a chance to know one another before you get lumbered with a baby.'

'I don't see it as being lumbered.'

'But you could always save for a bit couldn't you? And then you'd be able to get things that you wouldn't be able to do afterwards when you had to stop working.' When all else failed, one could always fall back on economic reasons.

'We have our flat and enough furniture to do. And Grandfather is always generous, you know that.'

'But you don't want to have to live off your grandfather.' I wouldn't settle for living off anybody. But perhaps in Catriona's family, where there was extra money floating about, things were different. It certainly wasn't like that in the McKinleys' household where we were fumbling along from one month's end to the next, often looking for money to pay the gas and the rent. The Frasers lived in a different world.

'I think it's better to have your children when you're young. And then you all grow up young together.'

I lay back on my elbows on the grass. A bee buzzed over my head, and the smell of rosemary and lavender was sweet. I could have lain right back and gone to sleep but it would hardly have been the thing to do when here was Catriona dying to tell me everything. And so she did, for the next hour or so, during which time I did my best to keep my mouth shut. If I'd said all the things I felt like saying we'd have ended up as sworn enemies.

Mrs Fraser came bustling out bearing mugs of coffee. 'You two girls having a nice little chat then?'

She gave us our coffee, pulled out a few weeds, and went back into the house. Through the sitting-room window I could see James's anxious face watching us from time to time. Was he hoping that Catriona might talk me into the idea of marriage? Surely not! Or put me off? More likely.

I let myself lie back on the ground. The sky above looked enormous, blue and fluffy white, and at the right side of my vision I could see a vapour trail, a thin snaky line of white marking the passage of an aeroplane. This was the day Phil and Mike were flying home. I took a deep breath, filling my lungs with all the gorgeous scents around me.

141

'Are you listening, Maggie?'

'Yes, I'm listening.'

Catriona resumed her tale. About Minorca. And her miscarriage.

Mrs Fraser reappeared, with a tartan travelling rug over her arm. 'The ground's damp, Maggie. You'll get your death of cold.'

I had to raise myself whilst she spread the rug on the ground for me, then I collapsed again. Sleep hovered, threatening to banish consciousness. Catriona's voice became fainter and fainter, like the waves of the sea, lulling and soothing me until I felt myself floating on the sweet air. I think I must have dropped off from time to time for I kept surfacing every time Catriona said, 'Are you listening, Maggie?'

After lunch, Catriona went to lie down for an hour, and James suggested a walk. I was dying to have a walk further up the glen but was reluctant to be alone with him.

As soon as we were ten yards along the road he said, 'Have you thought yet?'

'No.'

'Why not?'

'I hadn't time. We had loads of visitors in last night, Mrs Clark and Mr Farquharson—'

'But they didn't stay all night, did they? Didn't you think about it when you went to bed?'

'I was so tired I fell asleep at once.'

We passed the farm and came to the ruined cottage where my granny had grown up as a girl, the same cottage that Margaret Ross had come to after her long journey down from Easter Ross. The other end of the trail. Now I knew what both ends looked like. I ran across the field to it and sat on the window sill. James joined me. He took my hand in his.

'What are you afraid of, Maggie?'

'Things that go bump in the night. Daddy-long-legs.'

'Why do you never give an answer?'

'Why do you keep asking questions?'

'Because I want to know the answers.'

Fair enough I supposed, though I couldn't give them to him yet. Tomorrow, I told him, I would tell him tomorrow. On one condition: that he would lay off me today. He agreed.

We left the cottage and continued up to the head of the glen. We sat for a long time on a rock looking back down the glen, at the ruins of the old cottages, at the burn snaking its way through the heather, and at the hills on either side. If I had a glen in Scotland that I could call mine this was certainly it. Wherever I went in the world, and whatever I did, I knew that I would always return here. I said so to James.

'I feel the same way too, Maggie. You know I love the glen. It's another thing that we have in common. If we were to—'

'Now, now! You promised.'

He said he was sorry, he wouldn't do it again, would I forgive him? I did. We were at peace with one another that afternoon, not wanting to scrap or argue. It was certainly true that James and I got on very well together, that we enjoyed doing the same things, and were content with one another's company. That must be a good basis on which to start a marriage. If one wanted to start a marriage.

I stayed at the cottage for tea. After that Catriona was in a mood to talk again so we went to her room and sat on the bunks. She was restless, she said, and missing Alexander. Missing Alexander? Well, he was her husband after all.

'Wouldn't you like to be married, Maggie?'

'One of these days,' I sang, and added, 'Perhaps.'

'You always say things against it, don't you? Like getting married when you're ninety and there's nothing else going.'

I laughed. 'I say a lot of things, Catriona. Some of them I mean and some – well, I half-mean. But I'm not all that crazy about the idea of having babies.' That seemed to annoy Catriona though I didn't see why it should for I wasn't asking her not to have any, merely me. She said that I was unnatural in that way, that all women wanted to have children. I told her that was nonsense, that nowadays women could choose; they didn't feel there was pressure on them any longer to produce reams of children. I had given a five-minute talk at school about it. Five minutes had hardly been long enough for all that I could have said on the subject.

'But I think you *are* unnatural, Maggie,' said Catriona.

Was I? The thought did trouble me a bit, I have to admit, for nobody wants to feel they're unnatural, whatever that might be. I defended myself to Catriona, saying that she was conditioned into thinking that way, and that her children would not be the same. A new era was coming.

'So *you* say. But most girls—'

I was getting ratty now. I didn't care about most girls, I only cared about me in that context. I left Catriona, sought out James. At least he had promised to stay off that topic today.

He drove me back into town later to Granny's.

'See you tomorrow,' he said, before he left me, and his words were loaded with meaning.

I had to talk to someone now. I had talked enough to myself, too much, and was totally confused. It had been like a ding-dong battle raging through my head for the last two days.

I would talk to Granny because she was the only person I could think of talking to in these parts, or in any part, for that matter. If I had been in Glasgow I wouldn't have talked to my mother. Her reaction would have been predictable. She'd have been over the moon with delight at the prospect of me marrying James, she'd have considered him to be 'a good catch', and that in itself would have infuriated me. It would have been enough to make me reject James right out. And she would have been incensed to think I might pass up such a nice boy from such a good family with such good prospects in life. She wanted me to get married, she wanted to see me settled with some nice lad, and to give up all that silly notion of going to university and taking up that social whatever-it was. Aunt Jessie's attitude would have been the same, only filmed over with cloudy romanticism. Unromantic McKinley, is that me? Not completely. I do have my moments.

But Granny was different, she didn't think along a set line to begin with, she would sit and ponder and try to be as honest as she could. It was really no difficulty for her to be honest, it was her second nature.

When she had taken off her boots, put on her carpet slippers and settled by the fire, I took the chair opposite her.

'Granny, I'd like to talk to you about something.'

She looked up at me. 'It's about young Jamie, isn't it?' I nodded. She went on. 'I kent something was worrying you. I could tell by the look in your eye when you came back yesterday.'

It was easy to tell her, to explain my conflicting feelings, how I did feel really fond of James, in love with him even, and yet also didn't want to tie myself down, to give up the idea of my career. Granny herself had never had a career but could understand why I wanted one.

Funny in a way, when my mother couldn't.

'So you see,' I ended up, 'James is waiting for an answer tomorrow and I don't know what to say to him.'

For a while Granny was silent, and I almost wondered if she had gone to sleep. She sat with her hands clasped in her lap, chin sunk on chest, not moving. Eventually, she looked up again.

'Jamie's a fine young lad, and he'll be a fine man. He'll make a grand husband and a good father.'

All that I accepted, did not doubt for one moment. The question was did I want a grand husband and a good father?

'You're ower young to be married, and so is he, but if ye care for one another and ye wait too long, perhaps the time'll pass and never come again.'

I pondered on that, sensing again the truth of her words.

'But you seem to be a right clever lassie, Maggie, and you've done well at the school so it'd seem a pity not to go on and do this thing that you want to do.'

'It would, wouldn't it, Granny?'

'Do you have to choose between the two? Haven't you always been telling me that a woman can do both these days?'

Yes, a woman could, but there could be difficulties over our careers, I explained to her. James would have to stay in Scotland, at least for some years, until he was fully qualified.

'You've so much time, Maggie, to do everything you want. I'm sure you'll find a way to get it all fixed in. I wouldn't let James push you, and if he thinks enough of you he'll wait.'

She and her husband had courted for seven years before they married. I didn't think I was quite cut out for that.

146

'Remember that folk are more important than anything else in this world, Maggie,' said Granny. 'And now I think I'll be gettin' to my bed.'

I sat on by the fire watching it die out, listening to the faint moan of the wind in the chimney. Then I got up to fetch my rucksack. From it I took Margaret Ross's Cairngorm brooch, the broom-head, and the four stones that I had kept from Phil's collection. I laid them out on my knee. Objects. Not things to get too het up about perhaps, but all of them were related to people. In the career that I wanted to follow that was how it would be: all the objects, symbols, customs, that I would explore would lead directly back to people.

Phil and Mike would be back in Canada by now. It had been good meeting them, it had widened my horizons, as it were, given me something else to think about. In spite of my natural caution about things new, I do want to have wide horizons in my life; I just can't snatch at them too quickly.

On impulse, I left the house and went out to the phone box nearby. It was still only eleven o'clock, long before my family's bed-time.

My mother answered.

'What's new?' I asked.

'Nothing much really. We got an order in for a new bathroom suite today. Oh aye, and do you remember Isobel?'

Of course I remembered Isobel, we'd been friendly at primary school and together in secondary school, and then she had left at sixteen to start work.

'What's happened to her?'

'She's getting married. A week on Saturday. You've got an invite here.'

So Isobel was getting married too! It was starting to happen to a lot of my friends. By the time I was twenty I'd

147

be classed as an old maid. Not that that would worry me.

'Are ye no thinking about it yourself, Maggie?'

'Och, Mum!'

She didn't see why not, there was James such a nice laddie and clearly daft on me. And so on, and so on.

'Would you really like me to get married?'

She thought for a moment. So even she was torn two ways. I was glad of it rather. 'I'd miss you of course, Maggie.' And then slightly anxiously she added, '*Are* ye thinking about it?'

The pips went yet again so I said quickly, 'Must be going, Mum, or this'll clean you out completely.'

She let me go, with the thought of the telephone bill nudging her.

Granny heard me come in. The old devil that she is, she makes you feel you're inclined to rely on her hearing not being all that good, but she has the knack of catching anything she wants to hear.

'Maggie?' she called out. I went into her bedroom. 'Where have you been, lass?'

'I went to phone home.' I sat down on the chair beside her bed. 'Granny, do you think I'm unnatural?'

'Unnatural? Whatever are ye haverin' about now?'

'I mean, not being desperate to have a baby?'

In the dark, I could hear Granny chuckling. 'You're a daft bit lassie at times, Maggie. I never know what notion you'll get into your head next. There's nothin' one bit unnatural about you and I dare say some day you might want to have a child. But there's nothing unnatural that you don't want to have one yet. Why can't you be content to let things be and wait and see what happens? All this fuss to get moving on to the next thing!'

I kissed her. Somehow, in that moment, I had made up my mind what I would say to James. I daresay it wasn't just those few words that Granny said then, it was a result

148

of all the general mulling around in my brain that had gone on, and in my heart too. For, although I do like to play at being hard-bitten, that bit of me does work.

'Thanks, Gran,' I tucked her in, feeling very maternal, and giggled a bit inside me. Maybe I was cut out to look after old people. I get on well with James's grandfather too. 'Goodnight then, Gran. See you in the morning.'

Chapter 14

I lay awake for a long time preparing my answer to James. I imagined exactly what I would say to him and also, what he would say to me. The whole conversation went beautifully in my head. Of course when it came to the bit I forgot exactly what I had planned to say and, naturally, he did not say all the things that I would have liked him to say. In my would-be conversation, at the end, he had said, 'How wise you are, Maggie! I shall always value your wisdom and intelligence.' At the end of our real conversation he said to me, 'You are infuriating, Maggie McKinley. You always try to get out of taking a decision!'

'That's not true,' I cried. 'I have taken a decision, I've told you.'

'I know what you've told me. All you want to do is stall giving me an answer.'

'That's not true. I've asked you to wait another year and then we can see. What's so terrible about that? You'd think we were eighty, the way you go on.'

'I don't see any point in waiting.'

'Don't try to push me, James. There's no need to push in life. My granny was only saying so last night.'

So I'd talked to my granny had I? He wasn't exactly pleased about that, not that he had anything against my grandmother, but he said that he had refrained from speaking to *his* mother and father and that he had expected me not to take anyone into my confidence either. I sighed. I do seem to have the knack of doing the wrong thing, or at least of not knowing when to keep my mouth shut.

'I thought your granny would have been for me.'

'Oh she was, she was. She thinks you're great, you know that. But she doesn't think I should rush into anything yet.'

He said that he hadn't wanted me to rush into it at this moment, there was nearly another year to go. But he did want to get engaged to me.

'But why? Why can't we go on just as we were?'

He wanted to make it public, to show his claim to me, so that everybody would know. So that his mother would know in particular, I fancied. Couldn't I see that? We would then belong to one another, we would be committed.

Commitment. That's a big word, with a big meaning to it.

'Oh Maggie? Why can't you just say yes?' James caught hold of my hands and looked into my face.

I didn't know why, but I couldn't.

He sighed. 'Well look then, let's compromise. I won't say anything about it any more just now and you think about it and we might get engaged at Christmas. Okay?'

I agreed. Christmas was a long way off.

After lunch Mrs Fraser said, 'I feel like a wee walk, Maggie. What about you and I taking a turn over to the burn?' She wanted to have a wee talk with me, I knew that full well. I trotted by her side across the field down to the burn where the cows were drinking. Several of them were lovely shaggy Highland ones with sweet faces and spiky hair hanging over their eyes. For a few minutes we stood there watching them.

Mrs Fraser turned to look at me. 'What do you think of Catriona, Maggie?'

'She seems all right.'

Her mother shook her head. 'What a daft girl throwing her life away like that!'

'Oh I don't know. It's a bit early to say that, isn't it?'

'But to be married at her age! And to Alexander!'

'*She* must like him.'

'Now, Maggie, you know it was just that Alexander happened to be around at a certain time. I'm sure she didn't consciously *choose* him as a husband.'

I didn't argue any more, didn't think it would be worth the candle. Anyway, I didn't know what to think about Catriona and Alexander myself.

'I'm sure you wouldn't be so silly?' What did she expect me to tell her? Did she think we were going to have some kind of 'confessions' session? If so, she had another think coming.

'We can all make mistakes,' said I.

'So you admit Catriona made a mistake?'

I didn't admit anything at all. Mrs Fraser would have been good at the Inquisition, she could have got a first-class job.

'You will go on and have a career and make a good life for yourself, Maggie. I don't think you'll get married and have several children before you're twenty?'

If it had been anyone else I would have agreed wholeheartedly, certainly about not having kids before I was twenty. But whatever it is she does to me, I always want to say something that will worry her even more. So I said airily that we could be sure of absolutely nothing in life could we? Fate took unexpected turns at times.

'Fate, Maggie? You don't believe that fate will decide what you will do, do you? You'll decide that for yourself I'm sure.'

I was sick of thinking about my future. On Monday I would go back to school for another year, and that was as far into the future as I could gaze. If anyone was to offer me a crystal ball I'd smash it to bits immediately. That is, if you can smash crystal balls. I began to ponder on that, and Mrs Fraser looked annoyed because I wasn't listening to her now. She was still chuntering on, only this time she was actually mentioning James, and talking about his career and the length of time it would take before he actually got anywhere. I'd heard it before, so why should I have listened?

Before we left the cows and the burn, Mrs Fraser gave me a little lecture on the difficulties of marriage. She worked it in kind of innocently, as if it had just happened to crop up, but the gist of it was: don't! Did that mean that she had regretted being married herself? Tongue in cheek, assuming an air of innocence, I dared to ask her.

'Oh, not at all, Maggie. Well, of course Mr Fraser and I have had our ups and downs – who hasn't? – but we've managed to make a good go of things. I think I can say that. We didn't get married young of course: I was twenty-five and Peter twenty-seven. Those are more sensible ages. By that time you know what you want in life and who you are.'

I thought that sounded sensible, but again, I wouldn't have let her know that I did.

The rest of the time in Inverness-shire I spent with my granny. I washed and ironed all her clothes and Mr Farquharson's so that they wouldn't have to go to the launderette for a week or two. Then I baked a couple of cakes, tidied and vacuumed the sitting room and bedroom, and scrubbed out the kitchen. Maggie McKinley, paragon of domesticity!

'If you've a free minute my floor's gey dirty too, lass,' said Mr Farquharson, who stood at the open kitchen door watching me. 'You've plenty grease in yon elbow. You're young, mind, and that makes all the difference.'

I was a bit tired of being told I was young. Everyone used it in a different way, in the way that was most advantageous for them. Grumbling under my breath, I went off to Mr Farquharson's flat and scrubbed his kitchen floor. I doubted if it had been washed since the First World War. Kneeling on a wad of newspaper, I shoved my brush under the sink and into all the nasty corners, and wouldn't have been one bit surprised if a few snakes had jumped out and bitten me. The pong was horrible too, a mixture of sour milk and rotten vegetables, and heaven knows what else. I could have used a gas mask. I suggested to Mr Farquharson that he apply to the County Council for a Home Help, for people of his age who couldn't cope could get someone to help them.

'I dinne like strangers comin' into my house, lass. I manage just fine on my own.'

Well, everyone's idea of managing fine is different. I could see that every time I came up north now, I would not only have to do his washing, but scrub his kitchen floor as well.

'Is that scones you've been baking, Maggie? I'm right fond of a fresh scone. My good wife used to bake the best in the country, God rest her soul.'

He got some scones at tea-time, and in the evening we had a wee party. Mr Farquharson and Mrs Clark were there, some people from the town, and James and Catriona. James said that his mother was busy packing up the cottage so she sent apologies that she couldn't come, but she would be in to see Granny in the morning. We had a lively evening, with lots of laughing and talking, and even some singing.

'It'll be gey quiet for the next four months,' said Granny. 'I've enjoyed fine havin' Maggie here for the summer. She brings a bit of life to the place.'

'I'll be back at Hogmanay, Gran.'

'If we're all still here by then,' said Mr Farquharson mournfully. He was inclined to be droopy but I couldn't blame him for he lived alone and had no family to come and visit him. But I could have done without him voicing that particular sentiment for it was always one of my fears, that I might not see my granny again. Every time I left her the thought was in my mind.

'The lot of you'll see a hundred,' I said. 'You'll be getting telegrams from the Queen. So put that kind of nonsense out of your heads!'

After they had all gone away Granny and I sat on by the fire talking. She spoke of her granny and how she had told her the story of Margaret Ross. She had told me it all before of course but she liked to go over things again and again. And I liked to hear it too. It was comforting sitting there by the fire listening to her.

In the morning, the Frasers came to collect me.

'See you at Hogmanay then, Maggie. Take care of yoursel' and behave yoursel', mind! I see you have your Cairngorm brooch?'

I nodded. I put my hand over the brooch which was pinned to my shirt. My most precious possession.

'You take care of yourself, Gran. That's more important.'

We made as little fuss as possible at parting. We chaffed one another a bit, kissed quickly and then went out to the pavement. The Frasers' car was parked and waiting. Mr Farquharson and Mrs Clark were gathered already, ready for the big wave-off.

I squeezed myself in beside James and Catriona. Mr Fraser started up the engine; we waved, shouted goodbye, and then away we went, for yet another time, with the three old folk waving to us until we were out of sight.

The Frasers took me right into Glasgow. Being

Sunday, the shop was closed, but all my family was in upstairs. They weren't in because I was coming back, just because they were usually at home on a Sunday. When the car drew up outside my mother poked her head out of the window calling out, 'Is that you then, Maggie?'

Who else?

She came down to greet the Frasers and invite them in for a cup of tea but Mrs Fraser said that they'd better be getting along, they'd lots to do and she had to start school herself in the morning. She's a primary school teacher, and every day goes off to school loaded up with insects, leaves, sticks, stones; you name it, Mrs Fraser's got it in her bag. Her kids do so many projects that sometimes I wonder if they ever get time to learn that two and two makes four. In the boot of the car she had brought back half the glen, so that all our luggage had had to be strapped to the roof.

James got out of the car, and he and I walked along the road.

'When will I see you?' he asked.

'I don't know. When do you want to?'

'As soon as possible. What about next weekend? Come through to Edinburgh.'

I said I'd let him know. He pressed me a bit more so I said yes, I probably would come, but I would have to see how everything was with my folks and the business. Usually when I go away they get into a great muddle with the books and I have to sort the mess out.

'Your family seem to find you indispensable, Maggie!'

'Don't start that again, James!'

He said he was sorry, he shouldn't have said that. We went round the corner out of sight to kiss goodbye, then returned to the Frasers who were waiting to be off. I could see Mrs tapping her feet, metaphorically speaking, that is.

The Frasers went away, and I rejoined the bosom of my family. Aunt Jessie and Uncle Tam were in, come for their Sunday tea, with their several offspring playing around in the backyard.

Aunt Jessie wanted to hear all about the holiday, and, more importantly, all about James. She'd limited herself to waving to him out of the window and hadn't come down, probably because my father had told her not to. I gave them a gory description of our night out in the open, which sent Aunt Jessie into spasms of tutting and shaking her head.

'Trust you, Maggie!' said my mother.

'What do you mean, trust me? It wasn't my fault we got lost.'

'Maybe not, but things have a way of happening when you're around.'

It was nice being back. I like going away, but I also like coming back.

I didn't like getting up for school on the first morning. When my mother called me, I groaned and buried my head under the bedclothes. 'Get up, you'll be late for the school,' she shouted at me every five minutes for the next half-hour. 'Sandy and Jean are up and dressed already.'

I got up at the very last minute, flung on my clothes, pulled a comb through my hair and grabbed a roll that my mother held out to me as I ran past the kitchen. I galloped along the road, just missing a bus, and arrived late.

'A good beginning, Maggie,' said Mr Scott, laying on the sarcasm. 'Even though we have started an hour later for the first day.'

I made a face at him. Now that I was in the Sixth Year I felt that perhaps I could be allowed to show my feelings a little more. We didn't do any work that day, just got things sorted out, like timetables, books and so forth, and were dismissed early. I wandered home taking my time, knowing that as soon as I arrived I would be pounced on for something. I was.

'Ah, Maggie,' said my mother, 'it's great that you're home early the day. I have to go downtown with Aunt Jessie, so maybe you could just take over the shop for us? Oh by the way, there's a letter for you, one of those air mail letters with the red, white and blue round them.'

An air mail letter! I rushed upstairs and found it on the kitchen table lying under half a loaf and a dirty butter knife. It was indeed an air mail letter, from Canada.

I took it into my room, shut the door. Yes, it was from Phil, as I had known it must be. I had never seen his writing before, except for the little scrawl when he wrote out his name and address. I sat on the edge of the bed for a moment looking at the writing without reading it, wanting to delay for as long as possible the moment of actually reading it.

He said they'd had a good trip home, no hitches or delays or anything of the sort. He said they'd had a great holiday, they'd enjoyed Scotland especially, and it had been just grand meeting me. He hoped that James was all right now and fully recovered from his blow on the head and his cracked ribs. He sent his regards to James. He said that Mike sent his regards to me. He wondered if I'd managed to get all the stones safely back to Glasgow? And in conclusion, he said that he hoped I would write to him.

The letter was stilted and did not say so very much, but I read it over and over again.

My mother poked her head round the door. 'We're off then, Maggie. Don't forget the shop now!'

'I'm just going down.'

'Who's your letter from?'

'Oh, someone I met hostelling.'

She asked no more, she wasn't interested. If she had

known it was from another boy she would have stopped to give me a lecture on two-timing James and not throwing away something good when I had it. But I wasn't two-timing James, I'd only had a letter from a boy in Canada.

I went down to the shop, taking my letter with me. Business wasn't exactly hectic – I sold a couple of toilet rolls and a lavatory brush to two different women – so I had plenty of time to look at my letter and think about Phil. Would I write back to him? I wanted to, but should I? James didn't need to know of course, but if I started hiding things from him what would that do to our relationship? Honest McKinley! I didn't think I'd be any great hand at the deceiving game. I could imagine that before long, somehow or other, I would blurt out to James that I was corresponding with Phil, and that would certainly lead to a row. Should I then write to Phil and say I was sorry I couldn't write to him, that James objected? That sounded a bit daft. The only other thing was to ignore the letter completely, let it slide. But that didn't seem right either for I had been good friends with Phil and Mike, and we'd spent some very good days together. We'd been through a lot together. We'd spent a night in the church at Croick. And Phil had found my Cairngorm brooch. I chewed on the end of my biro. Another problem with no easy answer.

The door opened, and in came Janet Scott. I jumped up, pleased to see her, and made her a cup of coffee. Over the coffee I told her about my predicament.

'I don't see why you shouldn't write back,' said Janet, saying what I wanted her to say. 'It's not as if you're engaged to James.'

'He'd like me to be though.'

'Would he now? So he's actually proposed to you has he, Maggie? An old-fashioned proposal?'

'I don't know if it was old-fashioned or not but it was a

proposal. He wants me to marry him next year and get engaged at Christmas.'

'And what do you want?'

'I don't know.'

Janet laughed. 'I wouldn't have known either, Maggie, at your age. If I were you I would write to Phil if I felt like it. And say nothing to James.'

After she'd gone I ran quickly along to the Post Office and bought an air mail letter. When I came back there was my father going into the shop with his little plumber's bag, griping away about the shop being unattended and how we could have been burgled in the few minutes I'd left it.

'There's nothing much to burgle, Dad. A few lavatory brushes and toilet rolls—'

'What about all those copper pipes in the back shop? We'd lose a pretty penny if we had them snatched.'

'Somebody would need to be pretty quick off his mark to get these things out while I was away. Five minutes!'

My father grumbled on until I made him a cup of tea.

'What's this then?' He had picked up my letter which I had left open.

I grabbed it from him. 'It's mine.'

'Okay, no need to be so jumpy about it.' My father frowned. 'Who's it from then that you're so bothered about it?'

I informed him that it was my private business; he informed me that he wasn't interested in my business anyway. That was fine so then we got down to the plumbing business, which wasn't exactly booming. I told him that this was probably a slack time of the year for plumbing, when everyone was on holiday; also when the weather was good pipes didn't burst and things like that.

'Every time of the year's a slack time if you ask me.' My father's not the biggest optimist to be found in Glasgow.

He had another call to attend to so off he went, leaving me in peace to write to Phil. I told him that James was more or less recovered. I didn't tell him that I had had to dump most of his stones by the roadside. I said that I had enjoyed meeting them and sent my regards to Mike. Then I chewed the end of my biro some more. It wasn't a very scintillating letter but perhaps scintillating letters weren't what was called for at the moment. I concluded by saying that I hoped I would see them both again in Scotland some time. But I didn't say that I hoped he would write back. Somehow or other, I expected that he would.

I went to Edinburgh next weekend to see James, and he told me that he was going away for a month, to Italy. A friend of his grandfather's had a villa there and had invited him and his grandfather to come over. It was too good an opportunity to miss and he had about six weeks left before he started his university term.

'I still want to marry you, Maggie,' he said.

'Wait till Christmas,' I bleated.

James went to Italy, I returned to Glasgow.

'Italy?' said my Aunt Jessie, when I told her about James's holiday. 'They're not short of a penny or two in that family if you ask me, Maggie. You could do worse than—'

I interrupted her. 'Oh yes, I know what I could do worse than, Aunt Jessie. You and Mum never have anything else in your mind but money. Materialistic, that's what you are, both of you.'

'Just as well,' said my mother. 'Otherwise you wouldn't still be at the school at seventeen years of age, madam!'

I departed to my room, to escape any more of it. At regular intervals my mother went on about keeping me at my age, and always ended by telling me how she'd been out working at fourteen, as had my father and grandfather before him etc. It did lie uneasily on my conscience too at times, that I was still a burden to them when I needn't be, and all so that I could do what I wanted, to make a career that would mean nothing to them and bring them nothing in return. That was the way of it with children, I had tried to tell my mother, you couldn't expect returns back, but in her family and many others we knew the children did go out to work, to bring money in to help the family in return, so that in middle age the mothers and fathers weren't so hard pressed. I thought it a good idea, that they shouldn't be so hard pressed.

Again, that evening, whilst we were washing up together in the kitchen, my mother returned to the matter. 'What are you doing at school this year then, Maggie? You've got six Highers after all. You've said yourself that would take you into the university.'

'I've told you before, Mum, I'm doing Sixth Year Studies. That will give me a better background to go to university. It's kind of dealing with things in more detail. And I'm going to take a crash course in Spanish.'

My mother shook her head. 'I don't really see why you couldn't get a job this year, earn a bit of money and even put some by, and then go to university next year. You could do that couldn't you?'

I could.

'Well I think you should. The way things are going with money, we're finding everything gets tighter and tighter and it's more and more difficult to manage. Your dad's not getting any younger either, Maggie, so we could be doing with a wee bit of a hand. It's not as if I'm asking you to give up the university, though I can't really see what you want to be doing that kind of subject for anyway. But we'll let that go meantime. It's just that I think this year you could leave school and help us. Next year Sandy'll have left and that'll aye be one bringing in a wage.'

She really meant it, I could see that. She had probably meant it all the times before that she'd gone on about it, but this time it seemed to me that she was speaking with more purpose. She was asking me to leave school *now*.

She went off to bed, I went into the sitting room where my father was smoking a last cigarette before going to bed.

'Mum says she thinks I should leave school this year.'

He didn't answer for a moment, then said slowly, 'I think maybe you should, Maggie. Business is poor at the moment. I'm sorry to have to ask you. I'd like fine not to have had to, but I think I must.'

It seemed to me I was going to have no choice, not in this particular matter at any rate.

Chapter 15

In one way it was a relief not to be given any choice in the matter: I didn't have to take any more traumatic decisions. I'd had enough of them recently. But as soon as I was asked, or rather told to leave school, I realised that I didn't want to at all. I'd done plenty of moaning about school in my time, but when it came to the point I knew that I would rather have stayed on than not. I went to see Mr Scott.

'But this is ridiculous, Maggie!' he exploded. 'Your family doesn't seem to realise—'

'There's no point in them realising anything. They're in a bad way financially. And there's this new tax thing coming in for self-employed people, apart from everything else.'

We sat and stared at one another gloomily, and he, after his initial reaction, realised, too, that I didn't have a choice. He said that I might find it difficult when I went up to university after having had a year away from studying. I said I would just have to cope, wouldn't I? Of course it would be better to do Sixth Year Studies and go straight on to university. But maybe I'd been expecting too much, maybe I hadn't been particularly fair to my family either. I had to think about them too, didn't I? And for the four years that I was at university I wouldn't be able to do anything to help them. It was all right for people like James Fraser whose family didn't need help.

But mine did. And this Mr Scott could not deny.

It was something that had to be accepted. That I knew with the rational side of me, but it didn't stop me raging and storming at the unfairness of the world. I told myself that if this was the only unfairness I would have to gripe about then I would be dead lucky. What about all the people suffering in the Middle East and Ulster? And heaps of other places. Having an extra year at school was really like asking for gilt on your gingerbread. I mooched around the streets, hands stuck deep into the pockets of my jeans, scuffing my feet along the pavements, working the bile out of my system. There was no point in going home to take it out on them. They had done their best for me during the last seventeen years, tried to give me everything I needed, even if they hadn't thought I needed it.

It was typical of them though to have waited until this point to tell me. It would have been easier for me if I had known at the end of the summer term so that I could have got used to the idea, and also before I had started on my new year at school. In a moment of irritation I said this to my mother and she rounded on me saying that they hadn't wanted to tell me because they hadn't wanted to spoil the summer for me. I groaned. What was a summer compared with a whole year?

All the teachers at school lamented, after moaning at me for years! I told them my parents weren't being selfish or unreasonable, they thought it was I who was selfish because I wanted to spend years studying and not earning. The thought occurred to me that perhaps I should marry James next year, or even this year, so that I would cease to be a financial burden to them. The next moment I was horrified by the thought. Marry for money! Then I laughed at myself, which was what I was needing to do at that point. I'd been taking myself so gloomily and seriously that I hadn't seemed to realise that life wasn't coming to an end, it was merely taking another change and, as usual, it was taking me a little while to adjust to something new.

I dropped in at the Scotts'.

'That's it then,' I told them. 'From now on I have to be a working girl.'

'Have you thought what you might work at?' asked Janet.

Certainly not. One thing at a time was all I could cope with, and I had been so busy coping with the idea of leaving school that I hadn't thought beyond it. It was true enough though, that I should start to think about a job. But what could I do? I wasn't qualified for anything in particular, I had no secretarial training or diplomas of any kind, apart from my Highers, which weren't all that much use to anybody.

'I suppose you could always get a job in an office,' said Mr Scott. 'General clerking or something like that.'

Groan, groan! That didn't appeal to me at all. Could he see me in an office? I asked him. He admitted that it wasn't likely, I'd probably arrive late to begin with, lose all the files and spill tea over everybody.

Janet got out the paper and we studied the 'Situations Vacant'. We had quite a good laugh imagining me as a cinema usherette or toilet attendant or launderomat operator. Queen of the soap suds! I could just imagine me putting in three times too much soap powder and having a frothy flood over the laundry floor.

'You like debunking yourself don't you, Maggie?' said Mr Scott.

'Do I?' I smiled sweetly at him.

'What about helping out in a nursery school? Or a play group?' suggested Janet.

I made a face, I didn't fancy working with kids *en masse*.

There wasn't much money in those things either and I thought that I should try to get a job that was as well paid as possible so that I could give my folks some money and try to save some as well.

'That might mean working in a factory,' said Mr Scott.

I shrugged. Well, if that was what it had to be that is what it would be. I wasn't afraid of hard work. Ha ha! Maybe I was going to get a chance to find out.

That week was a killing one for me. I had the thought of James hanging over me, the thought of Phil in the back of my mind, and the problem of finding a job.

I had another letter from Phil; he must have written the moment he received mine. This letter was different from the first one, much less formal and cool. He told me what he had been doing, bits about his family, little stories, which made him come back to life again, and also made Canada seem more realistic. I sat reading the letter, thinking about Canada. It would be kind of nice to go there to work for the year. Why not? I could probably get a job that would pay me pretty well. I got quite carried away by the idea, was all but ready to set off downtown to book a passage, when I remembered my family. How I can forget them for more than five minutes at a time is beyond me! If I went to Canada it wouldn't do anything for them. They wanted me here, in Glasgow, earning a good wage which would help the family budget.

I didn't go to school that week, I couldn't face it. I went in to collect my books and say cheerio to teachers and friends, and the teachers gave me reading lists. They gave me little lectures too about not letting up this year, about doing all the necessary reading, and said that if I wanted any help I would know where to find them.

My mother laid off me, didn't nag me for not getting up early, and she didn't ask me to take over in the shop. She was watching me kind of warily out of the corner of her

167

eye. I have to admit that I did a fair amount of lying in bed in the mornings; the prospect of getting up wasn't all that alluring. I lay there thinking of James, as well as everything else. I got a letter from him too, from Florence. They were spending their days in the galleries. Great stuff if you can get it! No, I didn't feel bitter or resentful. What was the point? He was lucky in a different way from me but I wouldn't have changed places with anyone. In spite of everything, I've found it a great gas being Maggie McKinley. The arrogance of it!

I didn't write any letters that week. I re-read Phil's and James's several times. I kept them under my pillow. It seemed to me that if I went on and wrote again to Phil, who had urged me to at the end of his letter, then I would be developing my relationship with him. It was something I could develop if James wasn't there in a serious way. But at the moment he was.

When I did arise from my lowly couch, I went out job hunting. I put my name on the books of several agencies, went also to the Department of Employment. But I didn't fancy any of the things that they suggested; they kept telling me that in the first job I couldn't expect very much, etc., etc. I preferred to find my own job.

I answered one for a dentist's receptionist and he asked me to come for an interview. But as soon as I set foot over the door and heard the whirr of the drills I knew that it wasn't for me. Talk about me comforting nervous patients! They would need to comfort me. Next, I went round to a big hairdressing salon; they were looking for a receptionist also. They took one look at my tously head and said they would let me know, and as soon as they said it I sensed they didn't think I'd be much of an advertisement sitting in their front shop. I was relieved anyway, for the sight of lacquered women with boiled faces depresses me. I always feel they could find other ways of spending their time. Mr Scott told me not to be so puritanical.

'She's right to be so fussy though, Colin,' said Janet.

Each day I went round to them to report. My progress was not astronomical. I could always get a job as a check-out attendant in a supermarket; our local one was advertising for girls. I could sit there throwing tins into baskets, ringing up the money, boring myself rigid.

'You might just have to be bored you know,' said Mr Scott. 'You'll be lucky to find a job that you find interesting as well as lucrative.'

Factory work. It might have to be that after all. What a horrible ring it had to it! I imagined something Dickensian with machines clashing at a fearful rate, women working their fingers to the bone, deafened by noise, and some big man walking up and down cracking his whip. Twelve hours a day in the sweat shop. No, of course it wouldn't be like that, it would probably be all very civilised, with tea-breaks, and everybody having their heads wrapped up in scarves so that they didn't get their hair mangled in the machines. Things had come a long way no doubt.

'Factory work?' said my mother. 'You're not going to work in a factory! With all that education we've given you!'

'I have to go where the lolly is.'

'I'm sure you could get a nice wee job in a lawyer's office or an accountant's,' said Aunt Jessie. 'Something like that would suit you, Maggie. You're a smart lass and anyone would be pleased to have you.'

'You try telling them! If anyone took me on in an office it would be as a tea-girl.'

The trouble with my mother and Aunt Jessie was that they weren't up to date with the everyday working world. They imagined people would be beating down the doors to get at me, Maggie McKinley, just because I had six Highers. Even people with degrees sometimes found it difficult to get good jobs. Wrong thing to say!

'What on earth are you going to do a degree for then?' demanded my mother.

'Oh, social anthropology is quite different.'

Was that right now? I wasn't going to get off the hook too lightly. In what way? I declined to go into details. I said that I would probably work abroad anyway. I escaped out of the house, to do some more pounding around the streets, to read all the notices pinned on the shop windows, just in case some fabulous job was awaiting me. Assistant required, apply within. Most of them were being paid peanuts.

I went to consult my friend Isobel who had been working for over a year. She worked in a bookbinder's. She said, 'Why don't you come and get a job in our firm?'

The pay was pretty good, much better than any other job I had gone after. I said I'd think about it.

'I'll have a word with the Personnel Manageress if you like,' said Isobel.

So Isobel had her word and brought back the message that if I was interested I could come along to the factory for an interview. My mother was highly indignant, said I wasn't to go. It was all right for Isobel, she'd never had many brains, she'd left school the minute she could, and now here she was going to get married. But for me, Maggie McKinley, the top of the class, that wouldn't do at all!

I told my mother she'd never be satisfied, no matter what I did. Then I combed my hair, put on a coat instead of an anorak, and went round to the factory where Isobel worked.

The Personnel Manageress was dead nice. We had a long chat about this and that and I told her about my future aspirations (sounds great doesn't it?) and she said that she thought I might quite enjoy the work here, for at least it was more varied than in some other places. Also, and this was one thing that did appeal to me, they were working with books as end-products. I'd prefer to do that than work in a factory that was turning out toilet rolls or tins of cat food.

She took me for a tour around the factory floor. I saw the huge sheets of paper as they came in from the printers being put into the machines to be cut to the required size, then being bound together, and finally the jacket was put on and they were proper books. It was quite fascinating to watch all the processes, though I knew at the same time that it could become boring after a while doing the same thing day after day. But you never know, you might get a few books to take home with you. No harm in hoping.

It wasn't too noisy, and the whole thing looked much more congenial than I had imagined a factory would be. We'd once gone on a tour of a factory, some big engineering works, and the din and heat had been ghastly. I had tottered around with my hands over my ears, feeling thankful that I would never have to work in such a place.

After the tour we went back to the manageress's room. She said if I would like a job she'd take me on. I didn't stop to think. I said yes at once. It was time for me to stop dithering around and do something positive.

'Will you start on Monday then?'

Monday. On that day I would start work.

I rushed home to break the news to my family. My mother wasn't one bit pleased, as I'd expected. She moaned and groaned but I kept repeating the wage in her ear and that eventually quietened her down. She sniffed and said, 'Oh well, it'll do you in the meantime. Until something better turns up.'

171

That evening, I sat down and wrote to James in Italy. 'Dear James, I am starting work in a bookbinding factory next Monday.' That wouldn't half surprise him! I thought of him pounding the art galleries of Florence and Rome, filling in on his education, as his mother put it. Some day I would get there too, I didn't doubt that. I wrote him a cheerful letter, making fun of this new development, saying that by the time he came back I would have probably lopped off three fingers in the book slicing machine.

Then I wrote to Phil. When I had finished, I laid the two envelopes side by side on the dressing table. Jean, coming in to go to bed, eyed the envelopes and said, 'What are you up to, Maggie?' I told her to mind her own business. She giggled and read out, 'Mr Phil Ross.' I snatched the letters away. Having a younger sister is a real drag. I put the envelopes into a drawer. I still hadn't decided if I would post the letter to Phil or not. It depended on the decision I would take over James.

That was my last weekend of freedom before starting work. I did a lot of walking around the streets of Glasgow, in the parks, and the Botanic Gardens. And I thought a great deal about freedom. So I was starting work, giving up the easy day-to-day life I'd had at school where now, in retrospect, I realised I'd had a fair amount of freedom. I hadn't had to account for every minute of my day. But I wasn't going to moan about this unduly for it was only going to last for a year, and when that was up, I would go on to university as I had planned.

And now James? What of James? He was involved in my thoughts on freedom too. 'You mustn't think freedom is everything,' Mr Scott had said to me once when we were talking about it, 'You mustn't think it's all important. You must get it into perspective, see how much you want of it and what else you want in life. No one is really free anyway.' I knew that and didn't expect to be; it was all a matter of degree.

I really did care a lot for James, and this was making it harder. But I knew that, if I married him, I would have to compromise on my career, and it seemed ridiculous to set limits on it before I'd even begun. I wanted to travel, explore new places and peoples, see what the world had to offer. With James, all that would be restricted.

I couldn't marry him. Or get engaged. I didn't want a ring put on my finger that would bind me to him with a promise for the future. I knew it in my bones, and every other part of me.

I sat down on a bench under a tree. Some of the leaves were turning very slightly at the edges: autumn was on its way, another summer was over. I would have to say no to James, there was no other honest answer. I think I had known it for some time but I'd had to work my way through to being actually able to say the word, to make it final. For I had the feeling that it would be final if I said no. I didn't think he'd want me to go on with him as his steady girl friend. Maybe it wouldn't be possible anyway after all this, and I wasn't sure that I fancied being someone's steady girl any more. I didn't want all this emotional mish-mash. Soulful looks if you said the wrong thing, spoke to another boy, or even girl. I didn't want to be exclusive to anyone, not yet at least. I wanted to be able to write to another boy if I felt like it. To Phil. Yes, he attracted me. But he wasn't the reason I was rejecting James. I may not be cut out for fifty years of allegiance to one other human being, and if I married at eighteen, that was what it could be. If I'm not, then I can't help it; it seems to me that the main thing is to recognise it.

James wanted to be married, settled down, have his own house and possessions. I didn't want a house, didn't know what I'd begin to do with it, or possessions either.

173

They would just be a drag, get in the road if I wanted to move on or do something else. James and I were too different. I'd thought that before, but only in terms of things like class and background which now I saw mattered less than our attitudes, the way we tackled life.

I'd still like to see him from time to time but didn't know if he'd want to see me. He was going to be hurt and angry, perhaps even bitter at first. I felt a catch in my throat at the thought of not seeing him, at knowing that we wouldn't walk through the glen again, hand in hand, laughing, stopping to look at one another. For a moment I wavered. But no, I couldn't, I just couldn't.

I sat on under the tree till the air was quite cool. I sat thinking of James and Catriona and Alexander. It was funny, Catriona and Alexander had lasted longer than James and me, and I never would have thought it. It didn't mean that my relationship with James hadn't been as good as theirs, not at all. Ours had stayed fresh, we'd had a fantastic year, and I'd never forget it. And we had never bored one another. You couldn't say the same for Catriona and Alexander. What now for them? Well, that's up to them of course. I felt tempted to predict — Stop! It might last; they might change, grow together.

But as for me . . . I wanted to grow on my own. I was sad to know that it was over between James and me, I didn't feel one bit like dancing a jig down the path; but, after all, as my granny would have said if she'd been sitting on the bench beside me, I had my whole life ahead.

More Beaver Books

We hope you have enjoyed this Beaver Book. Here are some of the other titles:

The Clearance Maggie McKinley, lively sixteen-year-old Glasgow schoolgirl, spends the summer in a remote Scottish glen with her granny. She makes friends with the Frasers from Edinburgh and, partly as a result of this friendship, there is a terrible accident. . . . This is the first 'Maggie' book by Joan Lingard for older readers

The Beaver Book of Bikes A Beaver original. Packed with information on everything you need to know about bicycles – from buying, maintenance and restoration to games, activities and the history of bikes – this book is written by Harry Hossent and profusely illustrated with drawings and cartoons by Peter Gregory and Maggie Ling

The Beaver Book of Creepy Verse A Beaver original. A fascinating collection full of ghosts, ghouls, witches, monsters, ogres, spells and curses – some terrifying, some funny – and all guaranteed to send a shiver down your spine. Chosen by Ian and Zenka Woodward and chillingly illustrated by William Geldart

These and many other Beavers are available from your local bookshop or newsagent, or can be ordered direct from: Hamlyn Paperback Cash Sales, PO Box 11, Falmouth, Cornwall TR10 9EN. Send a cheque or postal order made payable to the Hamlyn Publishing Group, for the price of the book plus postage at the following rates:
UK: 45p for the first book, 20p for the second book, and 14p for each additional book ordered to a maximum charge of £1.63;
BFPO and Eire: 45p for the first book, 20p for the second book plus 14p per copy for the next 7 books and thereafter 8p per book;
OVERSEAS: 75p for the first book and 21p for each extra book.

New Beavers are published every month and if you would like the *Beaver Bulletin*, a newsletter which tells you about new books and gives a complete list of titles and prices, send a large stamped addressed envelope to:

Beaver Bulletin
The Hamlyn Group
Astronaut House
Feltham
Middlesex TW14 9AR

203018